LAND OF THE
BUFFALO BONES

THE DIARY OF
MARY ANN ELIZABETH RODGERS,
AN ENGLISH GIRL IN MINNESOTA

BY MARION DANE BAUER

Scholastic Inc. New York

THE JOURNEY TO AMERICA
1873

TUESDAY, 25 MARCH 1873

"The land is so rich, if you tickle it, it will smile a harvest." That's what Papa says, and Papa knows. You see, my papa is the Reverend Dr. George Rodgers, the leader of this entire colony. We are journeying, eighty of us, from our homes in England to Minnesota, one of the newest states in the United States of America.

Papa is our leader, because Papa is the only one who has seen Minnesota before. In fact, it is he who selected the spot for our new home. He and several other men traveled there last summer, brought by the Northern Pacific Railroad to scout out a place for us. When they returned to England, the other men went their various ways. They were afraid of this. They were worried about that. They thought not to like something else. Not one of them is with us today. Except for my papa. He is the only one who is not afraid.

And what could there possibly be to fear?

"The whole surface of the State is literally begemmed with innumerable lakes."

"Their picturesque beauty and loveliness, with their pebbly bottoms, transparent waters, wooded shores and sylvan associations, must be seen to be fully appreciated."

"There is no Western State better supplied with forests."

"The assertion that the climate of Minnesota is one of the healthiest in the world may be broadly and confidently made."

I copied all those pearls from a Northern Pacific Railroad brochure. Because Papa has done all the work of gathering this colony, the Northern Pacific is paying for our entire family to move to Minnesota, "begemmed with innumerable lakes," "supplied with forests." They are eager to have people populating their beautiful land, using their trains. And all who come with us will have first opportunity of selecting and purchasing farmlands or two building lots from the railroad.

"You bring the settlers," they told my papa, "and we will provide the town." And so we left the old Yeovil in England to make a new Yeovil in Minnesota. All eighty of us. And more to follow! Many more.

Back home, Papa put ads in the *Yeovil Western Gazette*. In one day, he said, a man could earn in Minnesota what he earns in a week in England. Clay County, he told them, is the best wheat-growing region in the United States. For the amount of a single year's rent in England, he said, a man could acquire a large and productive farm.

"The land is so rich," he said, again and again, "if you tickle it, it will smile a harvest."

How pleasant it shall be to see this new land. I am only a schoolgirl, yet perhaps I may tickle the land myself to see what harvest it will bring. Rubies and diamonds? Papa's words make such a thing seem almost possible.

But then what need have I for rubies and diamonds? I am the richest person on earth already. I am going to the New World! I am going with my papa to the New World! Has any girl ever been happier or more fortunate than I?

WEDNESDAY, 26 MARCH

When I began writing in this beautiful book Papa gave me to record our journey, I quite forgot to introduce myself. One never knows but that some stranger, years from now, may pick up this small volume and wonder at its author. Who is this girl? How old might she be? What are her dreams?

My name is Mary Ann Elizabeth Rodgers. But if you be reading this small book, you may call me Polly. That is what all call me who know me well. I am fourteen years, the oldest daughter of Dr. Rodgers, whom you have already met on these pages. I have four brothers, two half brothers, and two half sisters. My own mother, Mary Rodgers, died suddenly just a few months after my younger brother, Arthur Calvin, was born. I was but six years old at the time.

Little more than a year after my mother's death, my father married Emily Chant, who has provided him with four children more. Papa would like for me to call his wife Mama, but I do not. I remember my mama. And so because Papa would not approve of my saying "Emily" or "Mrs. Rodgers," the first not being properly respectful, the second being too distant, I have settled on Mother Rodgers. Such a name satisfies Papa well enough, and if it does not please her . . . well, that is her account, not mine.

She is, as I already made mention, not my mama, after all.

Thursday, 27 March

One would think, launched on the endless seas as we are, that a girl would have all the time in the world to write in a small diary, a gift from her papa to record this important time in her life.

One would think so, but it is not to be. I no more than get out the bottle of ink and dip my quill but that I hear,

"Polly, will you take Laura and Gladstone up to the deck for a walk?" "Polly, may I ask that you hold baby Percy while I nap?" "Polly, will you play with the children? Nellie is still ill today."

Nellie is the servant girl who came with us to help with the work of the journey and of the new land. She has been kecken-hearted since before the *City of Bristol* — that's the name of our ship — lifted anchor in Liverpool. And thus her duties fall to me. A woman of such refinement as Mother Rodgers, a teacher of French and music, could certainly not be expected to care for her own children all the long day! Though my mama did so. My mama never had help of any kind. Perhaps if she had, if her reserves of energy had not been so depleted when Cal was born, she would be making this journey with us today.

Papa's hair turned white overnight when Mama died. It remains white still. *She* has not been able to bring back its former hue. She has not brought back my heart, either. I believe I shall still be missing my mama's smile on the day I go to my Maker.

Cal is eight years old now, and, of course, was only a babe when our mama died, so he cannot remember her. Sometimes he even calls *her* Mama. "Mother Rodgers," I remind him often. But the next time he will say it again: "Mama."

Cal is part of the reason we are making this journey. He has been sickly his entire life. Papa has been told that the climate in Minnesota is a healthful one, that his son will prosper there. I hope it is so. For this journey does not agree with him, as it does not agree with Nellie, and it pains my heart to see his face so pale.

A sailor told us that sailors were once accustomed to drinking seawater every morning to keep from becoming seasick, but I haven't had the heart to offer such a cure to sweet Cal, and Nellie became indignant at the mere suggestion.

Despite all he must do, answering people's questions, soothing their fears, Papa comes by the cabin often to check on Cal. He holds a cool compress to my dear brother's brow, speaks a small prayer. But Cal curls into a ball on his narrow bunk that dips and lurches with the constant movement of this ship and seems barely to hear.

"Help your mother," Papa always says to me before he goes back out onto the deck to talk to the people he carries with him to this new place. "Stay close and help all you can."

And I do. It may be unseemly to say so, but I would help Lucifer himself if I could ease my dear brother's pain.

FRIDAY, 28 MARCH

Our fourth day on this ocean, and I take up my pen again, this time determined to fill these pages with the names of the others in my family. So here they be.

There are my oldest brothers, John William and George Newell, both of them grown. They are not with us on this ship but were among those who traveled with Papa when he went to discover a place in Minnesota for the colony. When Papa returned to England to gather the colony, both of them stayed behind in Minnesota, moving to other parts of the state to find work that suited them. I adore them both and wonder if I may be privileged to see them again. The place we are going to is so very large.

Next there is Frederick Luther, called Luther. He is sixteen and thinks he is a man, though there is much of the boy in him still. He loves to tease the way he loves to breathe and does both with equal ease. Still, he is my brother. That is enough.

Then, of course, comes eight-year-old Cal, the dearest of all. I am mother to him, have always been, as well as big sister.

After that begins Mother Rodgers's family.

First, Laura. Laura is five years old. She is a flibbertigibbet. Always underfoot. Always wanting her own way.

Always wanting to do whatever it is she sees me doing . . . except work, of course. I have to keep this book hidden from her. I saw her eyes when Papa gave it to me, saw them caressing the tawny, dimpled leather, the gold-tipped pages that bend as softly in my hands as though they had been made of silk. Her eyes said, "I want it. I will have it. It must be mine."

My eyes said back to her, "Just you try! See what will happen to you if you do!"

Papa understood none of this, of course. My father is a man of God, loving, wise, but entirely unschooled in the ways of the world. Mother Rodgers says he is made for higher things, and that must be true. Certainly he takes no notice of the lower ones such as sisterly quarrels.

After Laura comes Tom Gladstone, Glad, aged four. Despite his name he is a very serious boy, even solemn. We sometimes call him the little professor. Then Emily Augusta, called Millie, age three, all sunlight and laughter. And James Percy, newly born. It is too soon to know who Percy might be. All together I call them the littles. Laura hates to be included with the littles, but she is part of them nonetheless.

The littles surround me, follow me through my days.

Right now I am being surrounded, as usual, and must put my writing aside to take them up onto the deck before

Mother Rodgers complains of her head rattling from all their noise in our small cabin. I have heard the other women say that it was too soon for Mother Rodgers to travel after her confinement, but that she would not tell my father no. They said it is entirely clear that she knows not the meaning of the word when it comes to my father, but I hardly understand — or want to understand — their meaning.

Nellie yet lies with her head near a basin. Sweet Cal is no better. I sorrow for them both that the lovely swoop and sway of the ship should discomfort them so. There are few things I enjoy more than standing at the prow, feeling the boat's pitch and watching the endless ocean part before us. I have always loved the ocean, and once we reach Minnesota, which I understand to be far from any sea, I may never see it again. Thus I must fill myself with it now so that it may be a part of me forever.

So I put my pen down, my precious book away. I will take the littles up onto the deck. I content myself to know that the ocean will be waiting.

SATURDAY, 29 MARCH

These next are the borrowing days of March, said to be borrowed from April. But a cold wind blows across the

Atlantic, and I wonder that they might have been borrowed from February instead. A cold wind that makes for stiff waves. The waves do not help the ones who are ill.

Cal is no better. And Nellie, though she seems not nearly so ill as he, moans and carries on and talks about dying until the littles are frightened quite out of their wits. So to keep all calm, I have to hurry them away from the cabin and chatter brightly to them until my brain can scarce keep pace with my tongue.

Mother Rodgers stays quiet, just sits with Cal and with Nellie and looks quite pale herself. When I ask if she needs anything, she smiles and shakes her head, but her smile is pallid, and the shake of her head saying, "No, there is nothing I need" barely answers.

In all of this, of course, Luther is off and about the ship, probably getting into the way of the sailors who do the ship's work. We barely get a glimpse of him except in the dining salon. My big brother never misses an opportunity for a meal.

The worst of it, though, is Jane's little brother, Timmy. Oh dear . . . I haven't talked about Jane in these pages yet, have I? Jane Thompson is only my best and dearest friend. She is my heart, the reason I can face this journey with so little trepidation. She is fifteen to my fourteen. Sunshine to my shadow. Perfect obedience to my sometimes headstrong ways. If she had stayed behind, it would have been like leaving one of my limbs in England. But good fortune is with me. She and her mother and father and her younger brother — Timmy is seven — have come with us. All these past months Jane and I have thought about nothing, talked about nothing except this journey we would take together, what kind of lives we would make for ourselves in Minnesota.

Jane is a quiet girl, a respectful daughter, an attentive sister. I have often thought that Mother Rodgers must sometimes look at Jane and wish that Jane were her husband's daughter instead of me. But beneath that quiet is something more, something few know about besides me. Jane is restless, curious, eager to tackle the world. And she has as brave a heart as I have ever known. Braver than mine for certain. She even speaks with great eagerness about meeting the heathen savages in our new land. "Isn't it thrilling, Polly?" she says. "We will see real red-Indians!" Some days I wonder whether some parts of this journey, including "real red-Indians," might be just a tad more thrilling than I am prepared for, but I have only to clasp Jane's hand for my courage to return.

All is not entirely well, though, despite Jane's brave heart. Timmy, like Nellie and Cal, has been ill almost since we set foot on this ship. His illness, however, seems of a different kind, not just a sickness of the sea that will be over when his feet reach land again. It seems more and other, though what, no one can say. There is no physician on board this vessel, but the captain is much accustomed to dealing with illness. He comes and goes, checking on Timmy. Nonetheless, we worry. Even the captain seems not to know what to do.

The Lord's Day, 30 March

Jane, usually so full of laughter, has grown melancholy and silent with worry. Timmy does not improve.

Grandmother Chant has been often to doctor the child, too. On Friday and Saturday nights she sat up with him through the night after sending his parents to bed. Grandmother Chant is Mother Rodgers's mother. All call her Grandmother for her wise, good nature, so I call her that, too, though she is only a step-grandmother to me.

I, too, stopped by their cabin, though I knew there was little I could do. Jane's mother sat weeping, with her face buried in her apron. Her father was gone, off pacing the deck like a madman. Only Jane stayed close by Timmy's side, bathing his fevered brow, singing to him in her tender voice.

"Oh Jane!" I cried, when I saw the small flushed face,

the sunken eyes, and the restless hands plucking at the covers as though to throw them back and fly away from his sister's care.

But sweet Jane only put a finger to her lips and continued her song.

I left because services were about to commence on the deck. I spoke to Papa before he began, to tell him what I had seen, and he grew very still. Then he opened the service by praying long for Timmy.

Just as the service ended, word came back. Papa's prayers were not answered. Timmy is no more.

LATER

I went searching for Jane, but it was she who found me. "What shall we do?" she wept. "How shall we bury him? Surely we will take Timmy to Minnesota with us still. Shall we not?"

"Surely we will," I told her, but even as I spoke, I felt a deep foreboding.

When I carried the question to Papa, he shook his head and spoke the words I had been dreading. "We cannot wait so long," he said. "We must bury him as sailors have always been buried. Here at sea."

At sea! I could not believe such a thing possible.

Jane's mother has already lost three other little ones, each living only a short time after birth. Three who lie buried in English soil. Outside the churchyard, each one, because their parents are Baptists, dissenters — as we all are in this little group — and had thus earned these new little beings no place of rest in the consecrated ground of the Church of England.

How much worse, though, to leave Timmy behind in the sea, remembered by no stone, no mark of any kind. Can Papa consecrate the roiling, shifting water?

I ran back to Jane and held her in my arms and wept with her, but our tears were nothing to Timmy's mother's. She howled and wailed and tore her hair and even tried to rend her garments until Grandmother Chant and two of the other women took her away and gave her laudanum to make her sleep.

The funeral will be tomorrow. I still cannot believe that Papa can do such a thing, drop Timmy's dear little body — he has ginger curls, freckles, a sweet little upturned nose — into the hungry sea. I wish to be no part of it. I would go below and stay there through the service except that I must not leave Jane alone. Surely her mother is no use to her now, nor her father, either. He found spirits from one of the sailors and, though this entire colony is committed to abstinence, imbibed a goodly amount. Then, quite out of his mind with grief and drink, he stomped about the ship, blaming Papa for his son's death.

"If Dr. Rodgers hadn't put us on this ship," he kept saying. "If Dr. Rodgers hadn't put us on this rotten, filthy ship."

Papa's face grew very sad, but he said nothing to defend himself. Nothing about the fact that it was Mr. Thompson himself who chose this journey, that Papa neither forced nor lured him here.

Finally, when Jane's father grew more quiet, Papa took him aside and spoke to him, long and earnestly. I heard not what he said. And Mr. Thompson, for his part, threw Papa off at first saying, "Leave me alone!" and "Go to the devil, you." But then gradually he grew more subdued and when last I saw him, he was kneeling with Papa in a quiet corner and both were praying. So you can see from such an example that my papa has a powerful influence on the people here.

Jane, who watched it all, turned away, saying, "I wonder what good their prayers will do poor Timmy."

I told her that was a wicked thing to say. Timmy is with God now and has no need of our prayers. Prayers, Papa says, are for help for us fumbling humans, to keep us on the path.

Jane said only, "That must be true, for surely Timmy is beyond even God's help now."

In all the commotion, Laura opened the trunk that holds everyone's Sunday clothes — no one else had changed for the service — and got out her best hat and came up onto the deck wearing it. She hadn't been on deck more than three minutes when a wind came up and whipped that hat off her head and sent it sailing out over the shining water.

"My bonnet," she sobbed, as though her heart had sailed away with it. "My bonnet!" And then she turned to a sailor standing near and demanded that he fetch it for her. When he would not — could not, of course — she flew at him, pounding him with her small fists. Sometimes Laura's impetuous nature is a trial to me, but this time I gathered her into my arms and held her until her anger and grief had run its course.

Tomorrow we bury Timmy at sea.

MONDAY, 31 MARCH

This day was the saddest I have ever known. Papa held a service for Timmy, and all from the colony attended. Many of the other passengers on the ship came, too. "To honor a child they never knew, or for want of something more interesting to do?" Jane whispered to me, and I did not know what to say.

Papa says we must not judge others, that only God

knows what is in the heart. And though I know he speaks true, I did not say so to Jane. How could I?

Mrs. Thompson did not attend the service. She remained in her cabin and Grandmother Chant with her. Mr. Thompson came, but stood apart. I stood with my arm around Jane's waist during the entire time and sang with her,

All things bright and beautiful
All creatures great and small
All things wise and wonderful
The Lord God made them all.

And Timmy was beautiful. God had made him to be very beautiful.

Though why God took him home so soon is more than I, along with Jane, can imagine or understand.

When it came time to take that small body, sewn into a canvas shroud, and drop it over the side, Jane gasped and pulled away from my encircling arm. I thought she would follow Timmy over the railing, but Papa reached out and stopped her. For an instant she turned on him, eyes flashing, but then she caught herself and lowered her head meekly, obediently, like the good girl she has always been, and returned to my side.

Only she did not join in the next hymn.

Shall we gather at the river
Where bright angel feet have trod.
With its crystal tides forever
Flowing by the throne of God.

But it wasn't a friendly river that received Timmy. It was the dark, dark sea. He disappeared into that sea with only the smallest splash, the water folding over him smoothly as though he had never been.

Dear Timmy.

Poor Jane.

Tuesday, 1 April

April Fools' Day has come and gone, but the mood of all on the ship remained so dark that no one had the heart for pranks. Not even Luther.

I spend as much time as I can with Jane, but her mother does not leave off weeping and does not come out of their cabin, not even for meals, so Jane sits with her through the day and much of the night as well. Her father has not touched spirits again, but he paces the deck, his face stiff with sorrow, little use to either his wife or his daughter.

Last night I dreamed of the brine enfolding that small, canvas-covered package, and I woke, weeping. Cal crawled into my bunk with me and put his arms around my neck. Though there was scarce room for two to breathe in that small space, we slept that way the rest of the night.

Timmy was Cal's dearest chum, as Jane is mine.

REMEMBERING HOME

I remember gathering flowers with Jane. She knew each flower by its name, and in her hands every combination of color and style was made beautiful.

Poppies. Shy primroses. Hawthorne that blooms in May. Viper's bugloss and blackberry bramble. Bright holly berries.

There will never be a bouquet of flowers, the flowers of England or those of distant Minnesota, on dear Timmy's grave.

WEDNESDAY, 2 APRIL

We had midweek services this morning, though we had to have them in the dining salon because the deck was washed with wind and rain.

Papa spoke of God's grace. He reminded us that we had all, at first, been booked on another ship, the *Atlantic*, but that there had been too many of us to be accommodated there. So we had transferred our booking to the *City of*

Bristol, which now labored through the waters, holding us safe. He reminded us, too, what had been made known to us shortly before we boarded for our journey. Word had come back that the *Atlantic* went down off the coast of Nova Scotia, taking all 500 people to their deaths. So we must remember, he said, even as we grieve the loss of a precious child, that we are blessed in this journey.

God, Papa said, did not choose for those 500 to die, and for us to live, any more than he chose to take Timmy. He does not choose which vessel we board or which vessel founders, for that matter. He brings us into this world and then surrounds us with His love while we are here. And He is waiting for us when we leave.

That is all. And it is, Papa says, enough.

I write all this down as best I can, trying to remember Papa's words and to learn from them, but I find myself wondering still. What comfort did Papa's sermon bring to Timmy's family? None to Mrs. Thompson, I am certain, and Mr. Thompson remains remote and angry. I have not had the heart to ask Jane.

THURSDAY, 3 APRIL

This is the day! The day we will arrive in New York! I have spent hours helping to bathe the littles and getting them into clean clothes, packing away in our trunks every small thing we used while we were onboard. Except, of course, for Laura's Sunday hat.

I wonder if the fish have feasted on that hat by now. I wonder if the fish have feasted on . . . but no, I will not be pulled down by such thoughts. This is a happy day. I will see that it remains so.

I must go find Jane. I want to be standing with her at the prow of the ship when we see the new land for the first time.

FRIDAY, 4 APRIL

We are here. We are in the United States of America. And now on the train. The bumpy, jiggling, rattling, gritty, smoky, cold and hot train.

We went to a place called Castle Garden first, which seemed neither a castle nor a garden. It was a huge building set in a circle into which they herded everyone seeking admittance. Papa spoke for the colony, so we were all processed together. I was so proud watching Papa talk to the officials. Still they couldn't take Papa's word for everything and had to check each of us for good health.

The only trouble came when it was Mrs. Thompson's turn to be examined. She had hung back, waiting until last, and when brought before the physician, she began to wail.

She would not let the man near. Jane and Mr. Thompson were quite beside themselves, trying to calm her.

I think the officials might have turned Mrs. Thompson away as not being of sound mind if Papa had not talked and talked, explaining the poor woman's plight. Finally, the physician, quite disgusted he seemed, motioned for her to move on through, and that was that. All eighty of us had been approved to enter the United States of America.

New York City, though they say it is the largest city in these United States, is a ramshackle place. The wooden buildings look as though they were meant to be temporary and might fall down by the end of the day. Why, the huge signs slung up over the streets on wires seemed more substantial than some of the buildings. The place is teeming with people, though, and there are streetcars pulled by sixteen-horse teams! Hayburners, people call them for the deposits they leave behind on the streets. We were all glad to be out of there and to begin the second part of our journey on the train.

Some of the women, thinking we would be in Minnesota in but a few hours, put on their white dresses before boarding the train. After traveling all of one day and a night, we were told we were still many days away. And oh my, but those women are cross. Their white dresses are already soiled. Their clean white gloves are a fright! And everyone, dressed finely or no, is beginning to smell. It is too cold still to open the windows of the train, and when Luther opened one anyway, not being able to stand the stench of his surroundings any longer, the cinders from the smokestack filled the air. A live one landed on Laura's sleeve, and I had to beat it out while she caterwauled.

It will be a long journey.

SATURDAY, 5 APRIL

Sometimes Jane's mother sleeps and her father falls into silent brooding. Then she slips away and comes to our end of the railroad car. She helps me with the littles, especially Calvin. She cannot get enough of Calvin, but constantly reaches out to touch him, to smooth his hair.

If I were to pay such attentions to Calvin, he would throw off my invading hands with loud protests, but he accepts Jane's pats and caresses like a small puppy. He knows, I am certain, that her hands seek Timmy through him, and he remains perfectly compliant, letting Jane touch her fill.

THE LORD'S DAY, 6 APRIL

We celebrated the Lord's Day today, celebrated it rattling along in this train. Some folks wanted to stop, to do their hymn singing with their feet firmly on the ground. Some even said that the railroad should not be running at all on the Sabbath. But we took a vote and those who wanted to proceed won out, as Papa reminded us all that we did not depart the ship for the Sabbath. Also, we would have had to find hotels — and pay for them — if we had stopped off for the day.

We celebrated with hymns and with fine words from Papa about the coming Resurrection. He spoke about beginnings, about rising out of the tomb of the old life into the new.

I am ready for the new. I am ready! In seven more days we reach St. Paul, Minnesota. Seven more days!

I look back to where Jane sits, always holding her mother's hand, and every time I look, she smiles. I rejoice in the smile, though her eyes remain dark and still.

TUESDAY, 8 APRIL

The littles are restless and grumpy. Cal, though he is better for being on land, remains pale . . . and too quiet. I only hope that what Papa has said about the healthfulness of this new land is right, because I sometimes fear we will lose Cal the way we lost Timmy. And if God isn't the one who chooses such a loss, as Papa says, then whose fault would it be? Papa's for carrying his dear son so far from home?

Some of the people are beginning to grumble. They say Papa did not tell them that this country is so huge, that the journey would be so uncomfortable and take so long.

American railroad cars — they are called cars here, not carriages — are not divided into private compartments the way they are at home. Instead the entire car is open and filled with wooden benches, narrow seats with stiff wooden backs. A stove at each end makes the front and back of the car too hot, the middle too cold. Tallow candles make a dim religious light, but the odor of all these bodies does not bring religious thoughts.

This train carries a dining car that serves ten-course meals, but the Northern Pacific did not give our family money for such luxuries. Instead, we hurry off the train at stops and buy such food as we may to bring back and eat through the jiggling journey. Or sometimes we have thirty or thirty-five minutes to sit down and eat at a restaurant in the station. Often, though, the bell rings to warn us that the train will leave in five minutes when we have barely been served. When that happens, we must carry our food back onto the train anyhow or go without.

I can write only during the stops. I would have nothing but ink blots on the page if I were to try to write when the train is moving, and I often have to stop in the middle of a sentence when the whistle blows and then start up again at the next stop.

Thursday, 10 April

One wakes during the night and sees all the bodies draped over one another, children sometimes curled on the floor beneath the benches or in the aisle, and the whole place looks like a vision of hell.

Millie got sick all over my skirt and, scrub as I might, I cannot be rid of the smell.

Will we ever reach Minnesota?

Papa says we must be grateful for the great speed of this train. It forges along at a full twenty-one miles per hour. But I am so bruised from the wooden seats, so hot on one side, cold on the other, so tired of trying, without success, to keep the littles still and happy, that I cannot find anything close to gratitude in my bones.

I should like, at least, to be able to sit with Jane, but she must stay by her mother's side, and, of course, Mother Rodgers needs my help with the littles. I look back at Jane, dear Jane, and wish I could be as good and sweet as she. While I chafe at my small duties, she stays by her mother day and night, murmuring to her, consoling her, wiping her brow. But when we meet each other in the aisle or on another platform seeking food, she clasps my hand and some fire I cannot read leaps into her eyes.

Even on this interminable train ride Papa can find things to be grateful for. Why, just this morning he announced that if we had made this journey twenty years before, we would have left England on a sailing vessel and that the journey, just to the eastern shores of this land, would have required five weeks.

And once we had arrived, he told us, the rest of our journey would have taken many weeks, perhaps even months.

Even today, he said, there are many who launch themselves into the western world that is our destination behind a pair of oxen or horses.

Now that is something to be grateful for, not to be joggling along behind an ox or a horse. I have never much cared for any beast of such size, and I do not believe that riding behind a large rump, mile after mile, would change my mind about the matter.

FRIDAY, 11 APRIL

Today was the most glorious day! More glorious than any I have ever imagined. We arrived in St. Paul, and the St. George Society met us at the railroad station with a brass band. A brass band! Just think of it! And they tootled and sang and led us to a hall where they had a feast laid out for us.

The St. George Society is a group of English folk who live here in Minnesota. They were so glad that Papa is bringing such a large group over from their homeland — and will be bringing hundreds more in the next months — that they made a banquet for us all.

Such food! Venison, beef, chicken, sausages, roasted potatoes, carrots, marrows, apple pie, cherry pie, blueberry pie, cakes, piles of sweet whipped cream. The tables groaned with the bounty. More food than I can remember to record here. Certainly more than all of us together could manage to eat. Luther tried hard to do more than his share of the eating, but even he could make but a small dent in the feast laid out before us.

Then there were glorious speeches. How pleased they are that we have come . . . and in such numbers!

"We will wrest this state from the Swedes and the Norwegians and the Germans yet," they said. "We will make it fit to live in by filling it with good, solid English folk."

I heard Mr. Evans harumph at that. He is Welsh, and he would never, for any purpose whatsoever, call himself English.

The men giving speeches did not mention the savages,

wresting this state from the savages. Though Papa says we're not to call them that. "The red-Indians were here before we Europeans even knew this place existed," he said. "We owe them our respect."

The men asked us what we would do once we reached our destination, and everyone had an answer. All of the adults did, I mean. Of course, no one asked the children. Three spinsters said they are going to open a women's seminary. They said Papa had told them that doing so would be "as simple as climbing the studded stairs." One old man said his daughter was going to work in the millinery shop trimming hats, another that his daughter would play the "horgan" in the church. One younger man would seek employment killing pigs. It was what he did in England. One said he had brought with him a log chain to take down the trees he would be asked to fell in the park. Another had brought an engine with which to saw wood for the community. One was a tailor. Many said they were set to farm, though they had never farmed before. All were happy and excited, the long journey almost behind them.

During all the talk, Jane leaned toward me and whispered, "I think I shall find me a cowboy and wed him."

I could not help but giggle at the thought of Jane wed to a cowboy.

When the banqueting was over we bedded down for the

night at a convenient hotel, and though I could say more, though I could describe this hotel and the streets of St. Paul and the trees and the sky, I must not. Papa is calling me to snuff my candle and go to sleep, so I will.

Tomorrow we will be in our new home! How can anyone sleep?

P.S. Did you know that Minnesota is a Dakota Indian name meaning "land of the sky-colored waters"? One of the men told us that in his banquet speech. Land of the sky-colored waters! Could we have come to a better place?

EASTER DAY, 13 APRIL

Who would have thought it? Who could have dreamed such a thing? We arrived at our new home yesterday, leaving St. Paul in the early morning and arriving here in the evening after a journey of 253 miles. And yet we have seen nothing of New Yeovil still. Not a tree or a stone or a blade of grass. For there is nothing outside the window of our railroad car to see except snow!

That is what I said. Snow! And not sweetly falling flakes, either, such as we sometimes see in the coldest part of winter in England. This snow does not even fall. It flings itself horizontally across the earth until it strikes some surface that forces it to rise up, then settle to form a drift. Any surface at all, such as these railroad cars inside of which we are all huddled.

When we arrived here, the engine pulled our two cars and a third one that carries our belongings onto a sidetrack and moved on, leaving us behind. They could not stay, the conductors said, or they would be trapped in the blizzard. As we are. Trapped! We cannot even step outside the car for fear of having our breath snatched away, for fear of being buried alive.

A gowk's storm, we would call it in England. Days of tempestuous weather that come just when the cuckoo is first heard. But none in England has ever seen tempestuous weather such as this! And I would be surprised if any cuckoo would be foolish enough to inhabit this land.

The wind blows and rocks the cars until I wonder if Nellie and Cal won't grow seasick again. And the cold! The cold travels up through the wooden floors, in through the windows and walls. It passes through our feet, through our clothes, through our bones. The only way I can write at all is to keep the ink tucked inside my bodice to keep it from freezing and then, when I do want to write, to sit as close to the stove as possible. I must work in short patches, however.

The men keep stoking the stoves at each end of the car,

and Papa has worked out a rotation, so that every thirty minutes each family moves a seat closer or a seat farther away from the warmth the stoves afford. The men who are here without their families stay in the middle, farthest from the heat. If they have need of warming, they go stand in the aisle as close to one of the stoves as the crowd of children tumbling out of their seats will allow.

There is but little wood left to keep the stoves going. Food grows scarce, too. We have only some small amount of bread left and a few apples and water, melted from the snow. Even the tea that we brew is water-bewitched, having too much water for too little tea. The smaller children whimper with hunger. I cannot remember when I last saw sunny Millie smile; Glad is more quiet and solemn than ever, and Laura grows fretful and disagreeable. It is her way, I know, when she is frightened or sad to turn her bad feelings on me, but my patience wears thin. I cannot blame her, however. Even the adults are morose. And this day is so dark — and our tallow candles all used up — that I can scarce see to write these pages.

Another train should have come through today, bringing us wood and staples, but none has arrived. No doubt the storm has the next train stalled, as buried in snow as we are here.

And the next? And the next?

Have we traveled so far only to perish from hunger and cold on the very day our dear Lord defeated death?

Papa held Easter services here in our car, then went out to face the fierce wind and the stabbing snow to do the same in the other car.

I stood next to Jane during the service, piggybacking onto her clear sweet voice, for she has always sung truer than I. But even as I sang the joyous hymns of resurrection, I gazed through the window to the smothering snow.

When the service was over, Jane spoke softly so that only I might hear. "Might be," she said, "that your papa was mistaken in bringing us here to Minnesota."

Might be. Might be.

WEDNESDAY, APRIL 16

What kind of a place is this that cannot stop snowing and blowing though Easter is meant to bring a promise of spring?

The men have found a wooden fence not far from the tracks and broken it down and brought it into the cars to burn. They have taken up some of the ties that hold the rails on this siding, too. The fence, they said, is built by the railroad to catch the snow and keep it from drifting across the tracks.

" 'Tis called a snow fence," Jane whispered to me, and she giggled. The idea that we are burning a "snow fence" seemed to tickle her fancy. But I was too wappered even to have strength to join in her gentle amusement.

The Northern Pacific will not miss the fence. It did little to impede the snow anyway. When the flakes finally land, they do nothing but drift. Drift across the tracks. Drift across this featureless land. Drift up one side of this car until it shuts out what little light there is from the windows.

Today the snow has finally stopped falling, but the wind still blows and the snow still flies before it and piles against every obstruction. When the sun came out this morning, we could see the prairie for the first time. Such endless expanse of land. Such endless expanse of nothing!

And with the sun shining on all that white nothingness the reflection dazzles so painfully as to blind us all. As Jane already has done in private to me, people are beginning to murmur about a different kind of blindness, the blindness that brought us here.

We can make out three buildings. No more. Two, we are told, belong to the railroad company. The third is a small house, apparently the home of a settler who preceded us here. There is nothing else.

Where is the town we were promised? While we were

still in England, the Northern Pacific sent us a plat, marking the features of our town. Victoria Park, it had on it. Albert Square. And blocks and blocks of streets drawn upon the paper. How often Jane and I took out the plat to look it over, skipping our fingers from one street to the next. In our imaginations we walked beneath the trees in the park, sat in the square to watch the town go by.

"We shall be Americans!" Jane often said. "Citizens of New Yeovil, Minnesota, of the United States of America!" And she would clap her hands and do a little dance, right there before the plat.

But we are here now, and no town exists. Nor do the trees of our imagining. Nor the park and square of Northern Pacific's promise. No town at all.

Many who travel with us are filled with jangling talk about Papa. "How could he bring us to such a terrible place?" they say to one another. "Had he not been here himself to see, to know?"

But Papa was here last year in deep summer. He never saw such weather as this.

"Just wait," he tells them all. "The land will be verdant. It will teem with rich grasses, with crops. Just wait. Just wait."

He tells of the Baptist minister he met here who reported that one of his deacons had a potato cut to single eyes. When it was planted, he said, it yielded 92 pounds of potatoes. The deacon then took a third of an acre the next year and planted 75 pounds of potato on that and harvested 100 bushels. The potatoes were so large that 48 of them made a bushel, and one bushel basket weighed 60½ pounds.

But the people turn away, disbelieving. Perhaps not even caring if the words be true.

Still . . . there is naught for it but to wait. Wait for another train to come, bringing us food and fuel, wait for the sun to melt the snow. When the men step off the car to search for more wood, they are immediately up to their waists in snow. The littles want to play in it, but one step out of the car and they would all disappear, laughing Millie, solemn Glad, willful Laura. We wouldn't be able to find even the tops of their heads.

And so we sit on the hard slats of these benches, numb with cold, our bellies gnawing at our backbones.

Next, Papa says, we must start breaking up the benches we are sitting on for fuel.

I heard one of the women say we are all on a ninny-watch here. Could it be that she is right?

Remembering home

Easter. Warm rain falling, almost a mist. The world is green, green, green. Coming home from church to the warm brown smell of a roasting leg of lamb to be eaten with mint jelly.

We were all happy then, were we not?

I have forgotten. Why did we choose to come away?

Friday, 18 April

A train made it through to us today, bringing food and fuel. The people swarmed out of the car, thrashing through the snow to give the conductor a piece of their minds. Poor man. As though he had brought us the bad weather instead of the much-needed supplies.

Papa talked to him, too, patiently as always, and it was resolved that the train would take those who wished on to Glyndon, the next place along the tracks where there is a town already formed. There is a Colonists' Reception House there, built by the railroad to receive travelers, a newspaper, a church, a school, and nearly 100 settlers.

The train also brought us two large tents to shelter those who would remain. So we who chose to stay behind in

New Yeovil gathered our belongings and the babies and stepped down off the car. We stood in the now-soggy snow and watched what had been our home, however uncomfortable, pull away from us. Only the car holding our belongings was left behind.

I hope this shall not be the way of this harsh land, to find ourselves separating continually from whatever home we have endeavored to make, however poor it may be.

To my great gratitude, Jane and her parents remained behind, too. Though Jane still has little time available to spend with me — her mother continues to take up all her attention — I should not be able to face this barren place without my dear friend.

TUESDAY, 22 APRIL

The train that took some twenty-two of our party away also brought foodstuffs. And I have said already that it brought two large tents. One twenty-two feet, the other twenty-four feet square. I walked them off to count their size. The men have set them up and pulled trunks and bedsteads and chairs from the baggage car to provide the tents with small furnishings.

Seeing this accomplished, we all begin to feel better. Even Nellie, who has done nothing but complain since she left England, found the corner of the tent that was to be ours nearly acceptable.

One would think Nellie would have been grateful to have her feet, at last, on the earth when we disembarked from the ship, but she complained the entire way on the train, too, saying she felt almost as bad with the rattling and swaying as if she had still been on the water. She wept over missing her fiancé, too, who is set to follow later this summer, though what she thought to accomplish with her tears I cannot imagine. It isn't as though he might hear her grief and speed his coming. I have seen her fiancé, anyway, and would never weep over such as he. He has too much nose and too little chin for my taste, though perhaps he has other virtues I am unable to detect.

And so we set out to make our first home in this new world, though all continued in much discontent. Had there been a train going east that first day, I am certain many of our number would have been on it. But there was no such train, so folks who had not decided to go on to Glyndon had no choice but to stay here. They do have a choice about complaining, though, and they do much of that.

Mr. Thompson's voice is one of the loudest. Each time he speaks up, Jane bows her head and steps back, trying to disappear. Mrs. Thompson merely looks vacant, as though she has accomplished already what Jane only desires.

Must be we buried Mrs. Thompson's heart at sea with dear Timmy.

THURSDAY, 24 APRIL

The people demanded a meeting with Papa today to voice their complaints. And here are such protests as they spoke to him in that meeting.

First, they said they all had thought — as I must admit I had also — that we were coming to a town already risen from the soil. Papa answered that this fine group of men and women had only to put their minds and shoulders to the task and such a town would spring into existence. He reminded them all of the faith put in our small band by the members of the St. George Society in St. Paul.

Second, they complained that they found no trees — except on a narrow strip of land along the Buffalo River, and that strip could be the property of no man, because it was clearly subject to floods. From what, they demanded to know, were they to build their homes? Papa said the land being treeless was a blessing, that it would take a man and a stout horse or ox many years to clear enough farm acreage to sustain a family if the land be treed. How fortunate they were in these vast open spaces. They had only to set a plow upon the ground and it would open itself to their touch.

Third, the people said no God-fearing man would bring wife and children to a place where snow swirled through the air in such a fashion and at such a season. Papa answered that the storm was but the last breath of winter passing us by, and that they could see with their own eyes that all was now melting.

And they could, indeed, see. All about us were snow-bones. The snow was melting into sloughs, into swamps, into a mess of standing water and mud. However, Papa did not speak of sloughs or swamps or standing water. I am not sure, knowing Papa, that he even saw such things.

Many were unappeased by Papa's words, and when an eastbound train finally came, those who had sufficient funds were on it. Some to return to England itself. Some to find a more settled kind of place back east. Brainerd, perhaps, or Worthington, two well-established towns in Minnesota.

Others decided to stay. Some had no choice, as they had wives and children coming on the return trip of the *City of Bristol.* Or they had too little money to pay their passage back.

Some of the men signed on to work for the railroad. This work will earn them $2 a day for their labor, and it will also give their families a place in the Northern Pacific Section House here. Luther and Cal wanted to sign on, too, but there were enough men desiring the work that they had no need of a boy of sixteen and one of eight.

Papa, of course, did not go. He said his work is here among his people, even if many murmur to one another and no longer think themselves his people. Besides, Mother Rodgers says, one would never expect such labor from a minister of God.

It is a good thing one would not expect it, for I am certain Papa would never think of applying his hands in such a way!

Saturday, 26 April

Those who have funds have ordered lumber to be brought by train for building their homes. Since the wait will be long — none might arrive for a month — some who desired to build sooner found some settlers, not too distant, who would allow the use of their oxen . . . for a fee, of course. Thus they left our company to travel east to find lumber and float it back by the river. A difficult task, as the Buffalo River is running high, but they are determined to begin building.

Jane's father is among those who have gone after lumber. He must, he says, have Mrs. Thompson settled in her own house, and quickly. He is surely right, for after all these weeks and despite Jane's kindly efforts she does not leave off weeping.

If nothing else, settling Mrs. Thompson in a home of her own will mean that the rest of us will not be forced to listen to her grief, day after day and night after night. Sometimes I think I will weep myself at the sound.

Oh my! What a terrible thing I have written. I would take the words back if there were any way to do so. This black ink must needs remind me of the way thoughtless words, once brought into the world, may never be retrieved.

And if I am at my wits' end listening to the noise of Mrs. Thompson's grief, what must it be like for Jane, who strives constantly to comfort her mother, to urge her to take food and even to wash her face and comb the elf-locks out of her hair? Jane, who is herself grieving the loss of her dear brother.

I promise you, dear Diary, that you shall hear no complaint in these pages again from me . . . certainly not about Mrs. Thompson.

THE LORD'S DAY, 27 APRIL

Today after services came another meeting and the question of a house for our family. Clearly, Papa, who worked so hard gathering this colony and bringing us all here, cannot live forever in a corner of a tent while the rest build their homes. And clearly, too, the people cannot expect him to build for us himself. My father is a learned man, a wise man, but building houses is, I am quite certain, not one of his talents. In fact, I must say, I cannot imagine the dwelling we would have if we were dependent on his hands to devise it.

As a boy, Papa was apprenticed to a chair maker. He hated the work so roundly, however — and did so poorly at it — that when he got the call to preach instead, his master allowed Grandfather Rodgers to buy back the apprenticeship. He must, I suspect, have been well satisfied to be rid of his charge whose head was full of dreams and whose hands were often clumsy. Papa then attended seminary instead and was ordained at nineteen and for many years after was called "the boy preacher."

It is good that the chair maker allowed Grandfather Rodgers to buy back Papa's service. If there is any man who has no calling to be a chair maker — or a builder of houses — it is my father.

There was much discussion about what the people were obligated to provide for our family. If so many hadn't been angered at facing this bleak prairie after our long journey, the tone would surely have been different. As it was, harsh words were spoken. Yet Papa sat before them all, his hands folded, his expression peaceful and unchanging, as though it were someone else's fate, someone else's honor under discussion. I wondered sometimes if his ears could hear the words being said or their tone. Certainly Luther and Cal and I could. Mother Rodgers could as well. I saw what she heard in her eyes. Only the littles were unscathed. They are too young to pay much mind to the chattering of adults.

One man pointed out that a wooden house, 24 by 24 feet with four rooms, would cost upwards of $400 to build and that such a house would scarcely provide living space for so large a family. Another suggested that the number of the pastor's children was, after all, the pastor's concern, not theirs. When he said that, a glow of color dotted Mother Rodgers's cheeks, but she, like Papa, neither moved a muscle nor blinked an eye to contradict the angry speech. And then someone suggested that the best way to build a house without too much expense would be to build a soddy. He had been told, he said, that there were men in these parts who had the skill of such building.

I had never heard of a *soddy*. I don't know whether Papa had or not. But he rose and said only, "My family and I will be grateful for whatever house this congregation deems fit to provide," and he offered a prayer for all for our future in "this good land." Then he gathered up his family, and we left the meeting.

But my dear Diary, I wish I knew what is meant by a soddy!

MONDAY, 28 APRIL

This day I have discovered what a soddy is. It is a home built of sod that covers this prairie, built from bricks made from the top twelve or so inches where the tough prairie grasses hold the soil together. Cut damp and stacked on one another to create a dwelling, these bricks make a solid wall, good for many years.

When Mother Rodgers understood what our home will be made of, she wept. It was the first time I had ever seen her cry. "A house made of dirt?" she said to Papa.

"A house made of this good, rich earth," Papa corrected her gently. "And what could be better than a home formed from this fine land that has received us?"

I do not believe Mother Rodgers cared, at that moment, about this good, rich earth. In fact, I suspect she thought many things could be better than living in a soddy. One of them, perhaps, was even returning to our fine brick home in England. But she said only, "Pray forgive me, Dr. Rodgers. We will, of course, live as you deem fit."

It is a curious matter, though. "Dirt" and "good, rich earth" are but two different ways of saying the same thing, one being no better than the other. And yet the two sound so different. I should like to have Papa's gift of turning dirt into good, rich earth.

TUESDAY, 29 APRIL

The most terrible thing has happened this day. I can barely even gather the strength to write about it. I have told in these pages how far from herself Mrs. Thompson has come to be since Timmy's death, and though Jane tried always to stay by her and though even Mr. Thompson was solicitous and Grandmother Chant and the other women visited with her often, she grew more distant, more distracted every day. And she never left off weeping.

I have said, too, that Mr. Thompson left for Frazee to buy the lumber to build a house. A house of wood with "real windows," he promised Mrs. Thompson, "so you can hang gingham curtains for all to see."

But Mrs. Thompson did not wait to hang gingham curtains in her house of wood. She did not wait even for her husband's return. Instead she stole from the tent when all were asleep last night and went walking under the stars.

At first we thought that was all, that Mrs. Thompson had merely wandered onto the prairie in the dark and gone lost. And we all set out searching. But then someone found a scrap of her starched white nightgown, caught on a patch of brush. Another discovered the hymn book she had been carrying, dropped to the ground.

But it was Jane and I, searching together, who discovered the tracks leading directly to the Buffalo River. They marched right to the very edge and stopped there. Mrs. Thompson must have stood for a long time, watching the river tumble past, because the prints of her bare feet grew still and deep. And then they started up again and led directly into the water. Into the foaming, spring-swollen river. But not out again. Never to come out again.

Jane stood by my side, staring at this evidence of her mother's final journey and spoke not a word. What her face said, though, I could not begin to record here.

When all the community had gathered on the river-bank, coming to our call, Papa prayed. "Dear Lord," he said, "take this our sister to Your Bosom and keep her safe. Hold her and all her lost babes in Your Loving Arms."

Then he turned to the congregation and said, "If her body be found, she shall be buried in our new churchyard.

If it is not, we will yet erect a stone there in her loving memory."

There followed much whispering. The graveyard, some said, of our future church must not be contaminated by a suicide, a sinner. But Papa turned again. This time he did not call out in a strong voice, as he had prayed, but spoke quietly, so that everyone had to hush to hear his words.

"We are all Baptists here," he said, "religious dissenters. We come from a place that despised us for our faith. In our home country, notice of our marriages had to be made to the Guardians of the Poor in order that we might not forget our place. We were even refused final rest for our dead in the graveyards of the Church of England. Shall we then do to the family of this suffering woman what was done to us? Or knowing what we know, having lived what we have lived, shall we not begin this new day fresh?

"God's mercy extends to all of his children, but He must love most deeply those whose suffering is the greatest. Mrs. Thompson was and is loved. Let us remember that love."

And as it was in the story of those who sought to stone the woman taken in adultery and brought before Jesus the whisperers stole away, beginning with the oldest, down finally even to the very young.

Once more I held my dear Jane in my arms, though she brought forth no tears still. I wish she had.

Bitter or sweet, we are now part of this new land. It has been fed by our very flesh.

It was when we turned to make our way back from the river that we saw for the first time. As the snow withdraws, exposing the matted, tangled grass, exposing the dark earth beneath, something else is exposed as well. All this land on which we have come to settle — what my papa calls "this good, rich earth" — is covered deep with bones, whitening in the spring sun.

FRIDAY, 2 MAY

Mrs. Thompson's body washed up at a curve in the river-bank during the night and was brought home this morning. If this place can be called home. The men hastily built a coffin, using some of the wood Mr. Thompson had brought back for their new house. Then a spot was chosen in the 160 acres of land the Northern Pacific set aside for a church and churchyard, and a grave was dug. Papa held a service, and before the day was out, Jane's mother was buried.

When all was finished, Mr. Thompson got beastly drunk again. Though the law of this county forbids alcohol, which is one of the reasons Papa chose this place to be our home — he points out that in this bright clime a man has no need of drink to raise his spirits — Mr. Thompson had brought whiskey back from Frazee with his lumber. So Mr. Thompson got beastly drunk and roared and stomped and swore at Papa, blaming him once again for the loss of Timmy and now for the loss of his wife as well.

As usual, Papa said nothing, but later I saw him sitting on a fallen tree along the banks of the Buffalo River, his face buried in his hands.

Jane went off by herself, where I know not.

Since Jane did not seek my solace, I should, I know, have gone to sit with Papa, but I could not.

This day I have nothing more to tell.

SATURDAY, 3 MAY

As the snow recedes, exposing the earth, more of the bones Jane and I first saw are exposed as well. They are everywhere. One can hardly walk without stepping on them. They belong, we are told, to the buffalo that once populated this land by the millions. Papa says the beasts were slaughtered by white hunters who came before us and are coming here still. I try to imagine their living forms, their humped backs, their pounding hooves. They must have been fine to see.

And yet they are gone. Gone! I am told that only small

groups remain in this region now, and that they but seldom pass through.

The littles went out and began gathering the bones. They have managed a great pile. Laura says they are her toys, though how she means to play with them I cannot say. The children handle them as though they were, indeed, toys, of no more significance than a stick or a ball. For my part, though, the smallest glimpse of the piles they have made is enough to make me shudder.

I cannot help but be afraid. At least a little. Have we, too, brought death to this land? Will the land bring more death to us?

MONDAY, 5 MAY

George Chant, Mother Rodgers's father, has been appointed postmaster for New Yeovil. He intends, also, to build a store to provide the wares we will need to sustain our lives in this bleak land. All cannot be accomplished too soon.

TUESDAY, 6 MAY

In the night there are but few sounds. There is the wind, which never seems to stop blowing here. There is often the yelping of coyotes and the hooting of prairie owls, also.

The three combine to make a mournful melody.

But in the day, there is only the wind. No other sound at all. Who would ever have thought that the Land of Eden Papa brought us to would sing with such a mournful sound?

Wednesday, 7 May

This evening, just at the pinking in of the day, I looked up from grinding the wheat for our evening porridge to see a face at the flap of the tent. I would say it was a horrible face, for it was painted garishly, except for the fact that the man who presented the face was smiling. He also carried on his arm our small Millie, who had wandered from the tent when I should have been watching. Millie clung to the man's long braids and laughed and laughed, and he tossed back his head and laughed with her.

He set her on the ground, and then he was gone. We had no opportunity even to thank him.

I looked to Mother Rodgers. She was so pale I think she could not have spoken if the red-Indian man had been about to eat Millie instead of delivering her to us safe and whole.

It is the first we have seen of this race, though I think it will not be the last. I am sorry that Jane was off with her father and not here to meet her first savage.

THURSDAY, 8 MAY

Many have ordered lumber to be brought on the train, and they look hard for it to arrive. Jane's father has begun work with the lumber he has already secured to build a small frame house. They need but little space with only the two left in their family.

As he is so occupied, Jane is left on her own and comes often to help me with my work, or sometimes we seek Mother Rodgers's permission that the two of us may walk a ways together. We find little to say these days, not like the old when we chattered almost without stop. Still, it is good to walk out side by side.

Now that the snow is gone and the sun shines, the prairie grass leaps to life. Last year's grass lies across the prairie, brown and dead, crushed by the winter, but the new green shoots push up everywhere, thrusting through the old. Soon the grass will be so tall that even girls as near grown as we are could become lost in it in a trice.

Flowers bloom everywhere, and we gather them to carry back to the tent, though except for the yellow primrose, even Jane knows not their names. Jane sometimes grows excited again, seeing the flowers, and she will break away from me and run on ahead from this bloom to that, exclaiming, finding each one more cunning, more dear than the one before.

When she has gathered them into bouquets, I urge her to take one to her father, too, but she always declines.

"He has no use for such things," she says and leaves what she has composed with Mother Rodgers.

This world grows beautiful. The green land undulates in gentle waves so like a park in England that one expects, over the next rise, to come upon a manor. Still, the sky is so big, the sun so bright, that I return with relief to the dimness of the tent.

I am sorry it is the loss of her mother that has freed my dear Jane to come back to me, but I am grateful, nonetheless, to have her near. I daresay it is good for her, too. Yesterday she actually laughed when little Millie put Mother Rodgers's sauce pot on her head for a cap and got it stuck there.

SATURDAY, 10 MAY

Luther came home today with a catfish caught in the Buffalo River that surely weighed thirty pounds. Mother Rodgers was so amazed by the size, she could barely touch it. But when Luther set to cleaning it, cutting off great strips of glistening white flesh, she soon decided to make a fish stew for all to share.

Tuesday, 13 May

The second party of the colony arrived today, 120 men, women, and children. They were disappointed to find us living in tents, many others dispersed, much of the land still in a swampy condition, though men are working hard to drain it.

The men who have accompanied my father to this place are tradesmen, unaccustomed to such labor. Many have never wielded ax or saw or plow before now. Still, they go at the work with good hearts.

It has been discovered today, too, that much of the land promised to us by the Northern Pacific Railroad has been ceded to the ownership of the St. Paul and Pacific Railway and is not available for purchase.

Many of the second group dispersed before the sun had set. Only thirty-four remained in New Yeovil.

There is much muttering among those who remain, and I often hear Papa's name spoken with serious discontent.

Wednesday, 14 May

Some settlers passed through today, not by train but in covered wagons pulled by lumbering oxen. The littles and Cal and I ran out to greet them, begging them to stop their journey here, but they had their hopes set farther west.

They had a mother cat with them, a calico that, some weeks back, had delivered herself of four kittens. Laura admired the kittens so extravagantly that a small girl onboard gave her a ginger tom in exchange for Laura's best blue hair ribbon. Laura did not tell Mother Rodgers of the trade until the wagon had disappeared from sight, so nothing could be done but keep the kitten.

Mother Rodgers was not pleased. Unlike hair ribbons, kittens must be fed.

Laura named the kitten Pudding. I think she must be missing home to have come up with such a name. We have seen nothing like a pudding since our feet left English shores.

Remembering home

Menus for plain family dinners, copied from *Mrs. Beeton's Book of Cookery and Household Management* by

Isabella Mary Mayson Beeton, a book Mother Rodgers brought from home:

Sunday — vegetable marrow soup, roast lamb, mint sauce, French beans and potatoes, raspberry and currant tart, custard pudding.

Monday — cold lamb and salad, small meat pie, vegetable marrow and white sauce, lemon dumplings.

Tuesday — boiled mackerel, stewed loin of veal, French beans and potatoes, baked raspberry pudding.

Wednesday — vegetable soup, lamb cutlets and French beans, the remains of stewed shoulder of veal, mashed vegetable marrow, black-currant pudding.

Thursday — roast ribs of beef, Yorkshire pudding, French beans and potatoes, bread-and-butter pudding.

Friday — fried sole and melted butter, cold beef and salad, lamb cutlets and mashed potatoes, cauliflowers and white sauce instead of pudding.

Saturday — stewed beef and vegetables, with remains of cold beef, mutton pudding, macaroni and cheese.

A week's menus here:

Sunday — porridge made with wheat ground in the coffee mill and water.

Monday — porridge made with wheat ground in the coffee mill and water.

Tuesday — porridge made with wheat ground in the coffee mill and water.

Wednesday — porridge made with wheat ground in the coffee mill and water.

Thursday — porridge made with wheat ground in the coffee mill and water.

Friday — porridge made with wheat ground in the coffee mill and water.

Saturday — catfish stew, without the addition of either potatoes or vegetables of any other stripe.

I could wish for a goodly serving of blanks and prizes, a dish of beans with great morsels of bacon throughout. Or roast beef and Yorkshire pudding. Or even mashed vegetable marrow. Vegetable marrow is, I believe, called squash here.

Papa says we must dig a garden so as to vary our diet or none of us will be well, despite this fine climate.

He says this, and I suppose he is right, but I do not see him doing any digging.

THURSDAY, 15 MAY

This day we have begun to make a garden.

We had vegetables aplenty in England. Mother Rodgers

got them by walking around to the greengrocer in the morning. In the afternoon, her purchases were delivered to our house.

We had a garden there, too, but our garden was filled with flowers!

FRIDAY, 16 MAY

Plans are being made, in addition to Mr. Chant's store, for a blacksmith's shop, a carpenter shop, and a hotel. Mr. Chant's building will be manufactured by Bridges Manufacturing Company, of which he is the agent. He and Grandmother Chant will build a small frame house just to the north of the store.

Another man, Mr. Wilson, has declared himself a carpenter, too. He came by his profession this way: He decided on the journey over that he did not want to shoe an ox, so he was no blacksmith. There were, he could see when he got here, not enough houses to be painted, so he best not be a painter. He looked around at the land and said, "Can't raise nothing; it would freeze up, and besides, it takes money to buy a hoe." But he had a chest of tools from his brother-in-law, so he decided he was a carpenter.

THE LORD'S DAY, 18 MAY

Laura is a trial! We have our Sunday services in the tent, and with no wooden pews to hold her, she will not be still. And then there is little Millie, who titters at every wiggle of Laura's eyebrow, despite four-year-old Glad's sitting between them, as straight and stiff as a preacher himself.

Mother Rodgers is busy with baby Percy, and Nellie is off in her dream world — her fiancé is in it, I suppose — and sees nothing of what is going on, so it falls to me to keep them in line.

Papa, of course, sees none of it. When Laura runs up to him at the end of services, he always says, "Now, there is my fine girl," as though she had sat there like a lady the entire time. And then she turns and gives me an evil smirk.

If she is your fine girl, I want to ask, *then who am I*? But, of course, I do not.

MONDAY, 19 MAY

The men have started to build the church. When such is finished, it shall serve as a schoolhouse, too, though where we will find a schoolmaster no one has bothered to explain.

One of the reasons Papa wanted to bring his family here is for the free education, provided by the state, even through college. Our school in England cost twopence a week for each child. Here there shall be no charge, and every pupil is welcome.

But there is no school yet. Cal rejoices in his freedom from lessons, though I tell him to hold his tongue in his rejoicing lest Mother Rodgers decide to teach us herself. Perhaps, though, lessons would be no more onerous than a day of patching clothes, lugging water from the river, and then straining the critters out of it before boiling it over a fire.

We must strain critters out of the wheat, too. Our flour comes from the mill in Moorhead, but Mother Rodgers says it is clear they do not think to clean the grinder. I have heard said that, in addition to the grinders being dirty, the wheat, when it is ground, is dumped out onto the floor and gathered up from there with whatever debris might be about, then dumped back into the bags it was brought to the mill in, many of which contain bugs or dead mice.

If there were aught else to eat, I think I should eschew the flour entirely. Wheat flour sells for $3.50 per 100 pounds, though, so porridge shall be our meal. Sometimes we have cornmeal instead. It sells for 3 cents a pound in ten-pound lots.

TUESDAY, 20 MAY

Margaret Cecilia O'Donnell was born in the Section House this day. Her father works on the railroad. We have now had our first death and our first birth in this new land.

Does that mean we belong here now?

If we do, why do I not feel more at home?

P.S. This day is Laura's birthday, too. She is now six, though I do not suppose being a year older will improve either her disposition or her behavior. Luther had brought home eggs, gathered from prairie chicken nests, and Mother Rodgers fried some for Laura to celebrate her birthday. She ate them, every one, without offering anyone else a taste.

THURSDAY, 29 MAY

Last night we were all frightened quite out of our wits. Just approaching the time of darkness, a strange wailing began, an undulating call that moved up and down the scale in an eerie fashion. It went on and on.

"Wolves!" someone cried, and soon the children and many of the women were weeping and all were repeating, "Wolves!"

The sound was so close, we were certain we would be devoured in our beds.

This morning quiet had returned, so Jane and I walked out, as is our custom, though we walked with greater than usual caution. When we neared the Buffalo River, we heard the cry again. I gathered up my skirt and turned, ready to dash back toward the tents when Jane put a hand on my arm to stop me.

"Wait," she whispered. "Look!" And she stood transfixed, gazing toward the river.

I looked and saw a large bird, afloat on the water. It had black and white checks on its wings and a black head and neck with a white band around its throat and a strange red eye. When it opened its pointed beak, that wavering call issued forth. Another bird, looking just the same, answered from farther down the river. The sound was enough to make the skin crawl off my arms, but it came from a bird, no wolf.

We went back to tell the rest. Papa said the bird we described is a very ancient one and is called a loon.

If I had not seen the loons with my own eyes, I would have been certain still that we were going to be attacked and eaten in full morning light.

Since we are only girls and cannot be trusted to know what we have seen, there are some of our party who insist, still, that what we all heard was wolves lurking about.

"Wolves with feathers," Jane whispered to me. And she actually laughed.

TUESDAY, 3 JUNE

Today a settler living nearby named Mr. Swanson and several men from our colony began work on our soddy. I am determined to watch and to record all they do. Luther will work with them, so when I cannot understand what I am seeing, I can ask him to explain.

Building a soddy requires about an acre and a half of sod, Mr. Swanson told us. He has said, too, that the sod must be cut while it is still moist, but not too wet. That is why they have had to wait so long to begin building our house. First the sun had to drain away the standing water. And of course, too, the men had to take care of their own homes, their own families first.

Fall is really the best time to cut the sod, Mr. Swanson said, because by then the grass stems are woody and tough, so we must be grateful that we have not been told we must wait until fall to have a dwelling.

Before they began work, Mr. Swanson came to Mother Rodgers with a question. "Mrs. Rodgers," he said, "would you have a roof or a floor in your house?"

"A roof or a floor," she repeated, one hand flying to her throat. "A roof or a floor?"

"Yes, ma'am," he answered. "We have not lumber enough for both."

He explained that they could either put down a board floor or use the purchased boards to make a roof. If they did not put down a board floor, they would cut away the sod where they would build and pack the earth smooth. If they did not use the boards for the roof, they would build the roof from willow branches and cover the branches with grass and then with sod.

"You can tack up sheets inside," he explained, "especially over the stove, to catch sod bugs and snakes and the dirt that will trickle down from time to time. And to catch the wet when it rains."

Mother Rodgers gasped, but Mr. Swanson continued with his cheerful explanation. "When it rains, you see, the water will soak into the sod, and for the next three days or so it just might rain some inside your house."

"And people live this way?" Mother Rodgers asked. "On a dirt floor or with rain and insects coming through the roof?"

"Of course!" The man smiled. "Most folks live with both. It is your good fortune, madam, that we have enough lumber here for either a floor or a roof."

I could see what Mother Rodgers thought of her good fortune, but she drew herself tall and said, "I have brought my piano from England. Dr. Rodgers has his walnut writing desk. We have a fine bed that once belonged to my husband's mother. And a rocking chair to rock my babes. I will not have our possessions standing in the rain inside my own house."

And so the men went away to strip the sod and pack the soil for a dirt floor.

TUESDAY, 10 JUNE

Now I have watched the whole process, from beginning to end, and can record it here. First the men cut a day's worth of sod, using a cutter that looks like a child's sled. Then they haul it by wagon to the place where the house will be. Then they lay it, grass side down, in two or three rows, staggered. Every third or fourth layer they lay sod brick crosswise to bind the stacks together, and between each row sand is spread to make the fit tight.

When the walls reach two or three feet, the window frames are set and propped into place with sticks, and pegs are driven in to hold the windows in place. We are fortunate, we are told, to have four windows. Each eight-by-ten glass window costs $1.35. The lumber for the door, 54 cents. The door latch and hanging, 50 cents. The nails, 19½ cents a pound. A stovepipe, 30 cents.

The walls are sheared off on the inside and then plastered with mud and clay for a smooth surface. We can, we are told, paste up newspapers and magazines for wall covering. I think of the beautifully scrolled wallpaper in our home in England and smile, though I am hardly amused.

They set a loft, too, where Nellie and we children will bed down, except for baby Percy, who yet remains with his mother through the night. The loft, which is reached by a ladder, will be a good thing. The house is so small that if we were all to bed on the main floor, there should be room for aught there but beds.

No one mentioned the cost of the stove itself or the wood and tar cover for the roof. I would as soon not know. It is, I sometimes think, the curse of the clergyman's family to have an accounting of every detail of our lives made public.

The entire house is set to face south, aligned by the North Star. The sod is cut almost two feet wide, so the walls are two feet thick. The whole thing took a week to build. When the roof was on, and the door hung, Mr. Swanson escorted Mother Rodgers in to see her new dwelling.

"It will truly be the finest kind of dwelling," he told us. "Cool in summer. Warm in winter. Windproof, fireproof, bulletproof."

Mother Rodgers lifted her chin and put her hand on Mr. Swanson's arm and stepped into her new home like a queen surveying her palace.

I followed her and then we both stood there, staring . . . or trying to stare. It was the darkest house I have ever entered. Outside was full light, bright blue sky stretching so far and wide as to make one's head ache with the brilliance, but inside was only dark. The four windows were set so deep in the thick walls that even the summer sun could leak but dimly into the room.

"I wonder," Mother Rodgers said, "that we will have a perpetual blindman's holiday in this house."

"Always too dark to work," I added, knowing her meaning. "And too soon to light candles!"

Then we both looked around, walking from one corner of the dark abode to the next.

"Windproof," Mother Rodgers said at last, looking at me.

"Fireproof," I answered.

"Bulletproof!" we said together, and then we could not help but both begin to laugh.

What else could we do?

At least we will have a roof over our heads — one that will not leak, we hope — and a bit of privacy for our family.

REMEMBERING HOME

Our house in Yeovil was a fine brick one, narrow and tall, four stories. The bottom story stood halfway below ground level and held the kitchen, pantry, and scullery. A pump brought water to the kitchen and scullery. It was where Nellie prepared meals, washed up, and did laundry. Deliveries were made there.

The ground floor was several steps above street level. There was the dining room and Papa's study.

The drawing room stood on the first floor, what I understand is called the second floor here, and there the family gathered in the evenings. We entertained guests in the drawing room, too.

The bedrooms were on the floor above. My oldest brothers had their own rooms there, and Papa and Mother Rodgers shared a room with a dressing room for each on either side.

On the third floor was the nursery, where we children took our supper of bread and milk each evening — our main meal being at the noon of the day. There was a room for the boys and one for the girls, though often little Glad used to sneak into the girls' room and bed down with me.

In the attic above us was Nellie's room.

The windows in the front of the house looked out onto

the cobbled street and onto other houses as fine as our own. The ones in back opened to the garden, where flowers bloomed much of the year.

I think I shall never again see anything so fine. Strange that the house and all that was in it seemed quite ordinary when we lived there. Now, when I think about it, it seems almost too fine to be true.

Papa says we have learned appreciation in this new place, though I wonder if that is what we came for, to learn to appreciate all we left behind.

WEDNESDAY, 11 JUNE

This day Luther brought home an armload of fresh grass, and we spread it over the dirt floor. Jane stopped by to visit and said that no one ever had a sweeter-smelling carpet.

THURSDAY, 12 JUNE

Today I found Mother Rodgers clambering about on the roof of our soddy. It was a strange sight to see her with her skirts hiked up, walking upon the roof.

"What were you doing up there?" I asked when she was on the ground again, but she only smiled and did not answer except to say, "You shall see. Just wait. Soon you shall see."

Friday, 13 June

We have not had bread since we came here. Today Nellie taught Mother Rodgers how to bake bread. Nellie is a country girl and so knows such things. Mother Rodgers has had no need of bread baking until now, as she had a bakery from which to purchase such necessities. A quartern loaf of bread — just over 4¼ pounds — could be had for seven shillings.

Mother Rodgers and Nellie had set yeast to work two weeks before, since yeast cannot yet be purchased here. And the mere kneading of the dough took a whole hour. I could see by the time she was through that Mother Rodgers was near despair, but she did not say so.

Papa praised the result of her labor and Nellie's teaching, though I thought the results rather heavy and the crust somewhat burned. Still, we were all grateful to have bread instead of porridge. Would that there were milk to go with it, but that, I suppose, would require the help of a cow.

Many of the settlers who came here from Iowa and Wisconsin and other nearby places came by covered wagon instead of train. They have such beasts, but we have none here yet. I wish Papa would buy a cow to have milk and butter for our family, though a milk cow costs at least $30, so I might as well wish for the moon. I should be content.

If Papa were to find a way to buy a cow, the milking and churning would surely fall to me.

"Be content with what you have," as the rat said to the trap when he left his tail in it.

SATURDAY, 14 JUNE

Luther borrowed a gun and went hunting. He returned with several fat prairie chickens. They roasted up so fine. It is the first meat we have had for many weeks.

I had not thought my brother could accomplish such a thing.

TUESDAY, 17 JUNE

It is the Queen's weather, day after day. The sun shines endlessly, hot and bright, though Papa says the farmers will soon be wanting rain.

We find that this sod house, though not what any of our neighbors have, does have advantages. When the day grows hot, the air inside our dark cave of a house stays cool. As it will, we are promised, stay warm when the air outside is cold.

Wednesday, 18 June

Looking back at yesterday's entry, it occurs to me that I must take pains not to use expressions such as "the Queen's weather." In this land, of course, there is no queen. We say that at home for the fact that when Queen Victoria appears in public, she is often fortunate in having fine weather.

I wonder what days of sunshine and balmy air would properly be called here. President Grant's weather? I posed the question to Jane on our morning walk, and she said she fears that "President Grant's weather" does not have quite the same ring.

Friday, 20 June

Mr. Thompson is determined to establish a farm, though he never planted so much as a flower before coming here and it is late to start any crop. Before he could prepare his land with a plow, we children, Jane and I and sometimes Cal and the littles, too, scoured the land, gathering the bones of the dead buffalo. Pounds and pounds of bones, which Mr. Thompson will later sell to be ground for fertilizer. When that was done, he set to plowing with a plow called a sodbuster. For weeks you could see Jane's father bent over that plow from first light to well after the day's pinking in.

Jane always takes food and water to him at midday, but he will hardly stop even to eat or drink. Can you imagine sod so tough and thick as to be capable of making bricks to build a house? How difficult it must be to prepare such soil for planting!

Just yesterday, when Jane was taking her father his midday meal wrapped in a cloth, two red-Indians came galloping toward her. She dropped the food and the teapot and ran back to the house and bolted the door. While she watched from a window, those men dismounted their horses, unwrapped her father's dinner, and sat on the ground to eat it . . . every crumb. After sniffing at the teapot curiously, they even drank the tea right from the pot's spout. Then they left pot and cloth behind and rode off.

Jane waited for some time after they were gone, then went at last to rescue the teapot and cloth. Later, she stopped by to tell me that she had seen her first red-Indians.

"Did you like them?" I said. "Were they handsome?"

"I know not if they were handsome," she replied, blushing, "for I was running too fast to tell."

Saturday, 21 June

There are, we find, even more fearsome dangers to be faced in this land than the Red Devils, as many call the Indians hereabouts. The very land itself is an enemy.

Yesterday when Mr. Swanson was plowing, the ground opened up and swallowed his ox. The animal simply stepped into a soft spot and sank beneath the surface. Mr. Swanson had to go several miles to a neighbor to borrow a pair of oxen to pull his poor beast out.

Is there no end to the torments waiting for us here? Surely no one told Papa, while they were boasting of the number of bushels of potatoes to be gotten from planting one potato and the size the potatoes might be, that the ground itself on this prairie does not always hold.

Monday, 23 June

Mr. Thompson has finished plowing, and now he must drag the field to break up the clods of dirt he turned. He has no better tool for that than a large timber into which heavy spikes have been driven. He has recently bought a milk cow, and he attached her to this contraption and drove her back and forth across the field until the poor thing quit giving milk entirely.

Before the cow dried up from overwork, Jane made butter from the cream to sell at Chants' store, but she sometimes used to slip the buttermilk to us for the littles when Mr. Thompson was not watching. Millie cried for milk this eve.

WEDNESDAY, 25 JUNE

It is now time for Mr. Thompson to plant, and I had asked Jane if I could help. And though Mr. Thompson still will not speak to Papa, he is willing to accept the help of Papa's children. So he gave us, Jane and Luther and Cal and me, each a dibble, a pointed stick, and we spent a long day crawling across that wide field, poking a hole into the ground and dropping into each hole one grain of corn. Six inches away we would poke another hole and drop in another.

Jane and I grew weary with dragging our heavy skirts across the ground. "I have half a mind," she said at last, "to cast off this ridiculous skirt and petticoats and work in bloomers."

It is a good thing, though, that it was only half a mind. Her father, I think, would not have received well the sight of his only daughter, before God and everyone, in her bloomers.

We planted with the dibble all yesterday and today, too.

But late in the day today, a man came by on horseback. He sat watching us for a time, then began to laugh.

At the sound of the man's laughter, Mr. Thompson rose to his feet, ready to do battle. He probably would have, too, but the man had a long gun slung carelessly over his saddle.

"What are you planting?" the laughing man asked.

"Corn," Mr. Thompson replied, glowering.

"It don't look like corn to me," the man said.

"It is corn," Mr. Thompson insisted.

"Corn in the way you John Bulls call corn?" the man asked, a smile as long as a snake slipping across his face. "Is it what we Americans call wheat?"

"I suppose it is," Mr. Thompson said stubbornly.

And then the man laughed again. And laughed and laughed.

It seems we were planting entirely wrong. We were soon instructed that wheat, as the Americans call it, is planted by broadcasting, great handfuls of the seed flung out across the prepared ground, not by poking holes into the soil and dropping in a single grain.

Mr. Thompson disappeared this evening in a fury. Where he went I can only guess, and Jane will not speak of the possibilities.

Thursday, 26 June

When Mr. Thompson did not return by morning, Jane and I set out, carrying the seed in sacks over our shoulders and flinging it about on the turned land as the man had said we should do. By the time we were finished, though, I wondered if our first way hadn't been best.

From out of the empty sky, blackbirds suddenly appeared in great flocks, descending on the fields and gobbling up the seed almost as fast as we could spread it.

It is clear that a farmer's life is not going to be near so easy as Papa has promised. I have yet to see a harvest, but the work we have done has not felt much like tickling.

Because Mr. Thompson had still not returned, I asked Jane to come to us for tea, but she would not. She wanted to be at home should her father arrive.

It might have been better had she not been there. Mr. Thompson has, I have no doubt, found himself a blind pig, a place to serve him drink, illegal as such may be in this part of Clay County.

Saturday, 28 June

Our garden is coming up fast. Peas and beans and potatoes all well above ground.

The blackbirds did not get all of Mr. Thompson's wheat, for what remained has grown three inches above ground in but five days.

Papa was right about one thing. This land is rich.

Even the soil our soddy is made of is rich, for I have discovered at last what Mother Rodgers was doing upon the roof. She was spreading flower seeds she brought with her from England, and now our very roof is abloom!

MONDAY, 30 JUNE

This day geese came, flying over in great flocks, and they settled in the field and pulled up the sprouts of wheat. I have brought the littles to help, and Jane and I, Laura and Glad and Millie run into the field again and again, waving our arms and sending them off. Only to watch them settle and then to run again.

Millie went to sleep in the grass by the side of the field before I could bring her home for her evening tea.

We are all covered with bites from the mosquitoes and gnats. Which puts me in mind of something. Except for the blackbirds and the geese, both of which are only passing through, and the mosquitoes and gnats, which seem here to stay, we have seen few birds or even insects in this land since we arrived. All is, in fact, enormously quiet. Except for the wind.

The wind seems never to stop blowing.

Mr. Thompson has gone again, and this time he has been gone for several days. Jane says nothing of his absence. I asked if she would like to stay with us, but she refused with only a shake of her head.

I know what she would say if I asked further. She wants to be home when he returns. I only hope he is sober when he does.

Jane does not deserve to be so alone in the world. To have a mother dead and a father who imbibes spirits must be about the worst that could happen to a girl not yet full grown. Sweet Jane utters not a word of complaint, but I have only to look at her face to guess at the fierceness of her thoughts.

Tuesday, 1 July

The final group of our colony arrived today. They, as the previous group, came through the Great Lakes to Duluth and from there to us in Yeovil. The railroad station sign still says Hawley, but the post office is named Yeovil, which often causes misdirected mail.

Again, there was much commotion when they arrived, much talk and dissatisfaction, Papa in the midst of it all. It seems, in addition to all the other disappointments, that the Northern Pacific has deceived us about the size of the town lots. They promised that lots were 50 feet by 250 feet for $40 to $50. What people have found are lots they say are "grave size" — 25 feet by 150 feet for $80 to $100.

Again, many looked around and decided to move on to try other places, though the appearance of this place is much improved over what it was when we first came.

Nellie's fiancé was not among the travelers, though he had been expected. She has not stopped weeping since the train departed.

THURSDAY, 3 JULY

I examined my hands today, calloused with labor. Then I peered into a mirror to see my face, darkened by the sun despite the bonnet Mother Rodgers so often urges on me. In England I was hardly a lady. The daughter of a nonconformist minister would never be called such. But when I had a new frock — as I sometimes did — I did not look so very different from one. I could never be mistaken for a lady now.

In this place we hear the other settlers who are not of our

colony complaining of the fine ways of the English, even of our clothes. Mother Rodgers wears her black silk every day. It wears like iron, she says, and will outlast many cotton frocks. But I saw an American woman look her over and turn away, her mouth twisted in that disgust that is born of envy.

How strange it is. For we have given up everything pleasant and easy in our lives only to be looked down upon, once we arrived here, for having too much!

FRIDAY, 4 JULY

Today was a holiday, the first in our new country. It is Independence Day, the day in which these United States once declared themselves free of "British-tyranny."

That is the way they say it here, "British-tyranny." As though British and tyranny were one and the same.

The entire community stopped work, Germans and Swedes and Norwegians and Finns and English together, and gathered at Mather's Lake for a celebration. There were games — sack races and foot races and horse races — and music and even, when the dark came up, some banging fireworks, brought on the train from the East. And there were speeches. Loud speeches. Speeches boasting of this America as the finest land on earth.

I wonder that these Americans do not make all things common by speaking of them so openly and in such grand terms.

Some of the Ojibwa, the name for the red-Indian people who have long lived here, put in an appearance and danced for us, though what they were celebrating I could not say. Jane moved to the edge of the circle of watchers and stood as one entranced.

"Jane," I said once, tugging on her sleeve, "you are staring!"

To my surprise, she paid me no mind. In fact, she shook off my hand and went right on gazing in that steadfast way.

Then began more speeches, and a sudden thunderstorm came up while they were still going on, louder than the fireworks that were to follow, and soaked us all in our best clothes.

Still the fireworks went on when the storm had rumbled past.

When all was over, our family walked slowly back to our small sod house. The littles dragged their feet or slept in the arms of someone strong enough to carry them. And Papa said, "Well, then, I suppose we must all be Americans now. We have celebrated our independence from England."

But as I climbed the ladder to the loft with Millie's curly head lolling on my shoulder, I wondered. Must independence come at such a cost?

And do I want to be an American?

Truly?

TUESDAY, 8 JULY

The Union Church was formed this day, a church that will be open to all who love the Savior, whatever be their denomination. As yet Papa has not been elected its pastor, and no salary has been fixed for the man they will call. I overheard Papa and Mother Rodgers talking, and thus I know that now that all the colony is gathered, such as it is, the Northern Pacific Railroad no longer pays him a small wage.

Papa says, "The Lord will provide." Mother Rodgers says nothing to contradict her husband, though I can see from the set of her jaw that she would prefer to rely on a salary, however, small, than on the generosity of the Lord.

I cannot say that I blame her. After all, look at the manner in which He provided for His own Son!

REMEMBERING HOME

Papa's last church wasn't in Yeovil, in Somerset, the place from which we have emigrated. It was a bit farther east in Stalbridge, in the county of Dorset. Stalbridge is a fine place, a village set in the midst of good, rich farmland. Thus the more well-to-do of the congregation were farmers. Many of the less well-to-do were those who worked on the farms.

My father is a man of great principle, and when the labor unions began soliciting membership from farm laborers, Papa spoke from the pulpit in favor of the unions. The farmers grumbled in their pews, but they let the matter pass.

When Papa began talking to the farmworkers about how much better their lives would be in the north of England, the farmers' consternation was complete. They withdrew their support from the church, and without their support the church became very poor indeed. Thus, Papa resigned, not wishing to take the congregation down with him, and that was when we moved to Yeovil, which had been Mother Rodgers's home. It was only natural then, having no church, that Papa should make an agreement with the Northern Pacific Railroad to gather a colony to bring here. What better way to help the suffering farmworkers than to bring them to this new and rich land?

Though it isn't farmworkers who answered the call so much as tradesmen. How could farmworkers ever get money together from their meager incomes to make such a journey?

I was proud of my papa all that time. Very proud. Not every man — not even every minister — has the courage to stand for what he truly believes when his beliefs will be an inconvenience to him and to those he loves.

I am proud of him still. Sometimes, though, I cannot help but remember the days in Stalbridge. In my mind I stand looking out from the edge of town at the green land, the gentle sheep dotting the pastures, the stone walls marking it off like frames for a picture.

Papa says those walls, however charming they might look, were the beginning of the subjugation of the farmworkers. They divided off the countryside for the rich landowners, leaving little or nothing in common on which the poor could graze their few beasts. Papa says England is a used-up kind of place, every inch parceled out again and again. Here, he says, a man may make a fresh start and reap whatever his own labor can sow. Here, he says, land is available for all. And he is right.

Of course.

Papa is right.

Only what good is land to those of us who know so little of farming that we use a dibble to plant what these Americans call wheat?

THURSDAY, 10 JULY

Today Jane and I found wild strawberries, sweet and ripe. We picked them and carried them home in our aprons, and all ate and ate until every lip was stained bright with sweetness. When she left to go home, Jane even carried some of the bright berries to her father.

FRIDAY, 11 JULY

The strangest thing happened to Jane and to me this day. So strange I must pause before I can put pen to page. It is as though we were both caught in a dream, but one of Jane's making, not mine.

We were walking as we often do in the early morning along the banks of the Buffalo River. As I have told before, it is treed there, mostly willows and other slender, scrubby trees, the only ones we ever see on this prairie. Because of the trees and underbrush we could not see far ahead or around us. Thus when I first heard the high mournful howl, which made the fine hairs on the back of my neck stand to attention, I could see nothing either before or behind that might be the source of the sound.

Jane grew pale. She has been looking quite wappered lately — even more than when she was watching over her mother so constantly — but when I ask what the trouble is, she smiles and says there is no trouble. This time, though, her face turned positively white.

"It is those birds," I said, putting a hand on her arm to assure her. "The ones Papa called loons."

"Of course," she said. "Certainly, it is loons."

But then the howling took up again, even closer this time. Closer than the riverbank, which was yet many yards away. And not only did the sound come from behind us, but it came from before and beside us as well. It was clear that whatever was making the noise did not swim on the water, but moved on land, and it wailed its eerie, undulating call from every side.

We clung to each other, looking this way and that, trembling. And then I saw, as I gazed over Jane's shoulder, the thing I had feared above all else. A great gray beast skulked just beyond the nearest trees. And turning I saw another and another. We were surrounded! The wolves — for that is what they were this time, no loons — moved in a circle with us forming the center, howling and howling.

I told Jane what I saw, hoping she would say I was dreaming, but by this time she had seen, too. We both knew for a certainty that in the next moment we would be attacked and the flesh ripped from our bones. I even thought to wonder whether there would be enough left of us for our families to bury or if our bones would end up mingled with those of the buffalo that cover this desolate prairie.

Jane and I knelt together, our arms still tightly circling each other, and began to pray. Or rather Jane prayed. My throat had gone so dry that I could utter no sound.

"Dear Lord," Jane said, "if this be the end, please take us quickly to Your Bosom. Let us not feel the pain."

And I thought, *No! Don't pray such! Ask that the wolves may die instead!* I said none of that, though, because still I could find no voice. Perhaps it is just as well. The Lord of Creation might not look favorably upon being asked to strike down His own creatures merely for doing what they were meant to do — seeking food. Though surely He did not make Jane and me only to satisfy their beastly appetites!

We quavered, we wept, and the wolves circled and circled on silent paws. Only their voices were not silent. They howled, their voices rising and rising, twining about one another until they sounded like ten wolves, like twenty.

Then another thing happened, a thing so startling as almost to be worse than being surrounded by wolves in this bit of woods. A man stepped out from behind a close stand of willows, a young red-Indian man. He was oddly dressed, wearing a coat and shirt, in imitation of the clothes of any white settler, but he also had on fringed leggings bound around the knee with bead bands, a breechcloth, woven sash, and moccasins, the clothes of a savage. The style of his hair, too, went with his southern parts, for it fell in two long, black braids.

He did not speak, but put one dark hand on Jane's shoulder, one on mine, and motioned for us to follow him.

Despite our terror — or perhaps because of it — we did as we were bidden. We struggled to stand from where we knelt, and that stranger, with one of us at each side, turned and walked through the circle of wolves as though he were Moses come to part the Red Sea. When we had moved out of the trees, a distance past that deadly circle, he stopped to speak to us.

"Wolves have no taste for human flesh," he said. "They would not have harmed you."

I wanted to ask a thousand questions . . . about the wolves, about him, but I had no voice. Apparently Jane had none either, for she, too, was silent.

Next the young man — I almost wrote "the young savage," but surely he did not have the manner of a savage — said, "Come back tomorrow. Come to this place at this same time in the morning. I will show you why the wolves sang to you."

And then he was gone. He turned back into the woods and disappeared. He must have had a horse waiting, for soon we saw a horse and rider emerge from the trees farther along the bank.

For a long moment Jane and I stood like stones watching the dust of the horse's departure.

"There is the red-Indian you longed to meet," I told her. Then, on a single impulse, we grasped hands fiercely and ran back in the direction of the sod hut. We arrived inside the door, gasping for breath, and Mother Rodgers, who sat in the rocking chair brought from England, feeding baby Percy, looked up and frowned.

"Girls," she admonished us both, "you have forgotten yourselves. Ladies do not run."

Since Jane is now as without a mother as I am, Mother Rodgers deems it her responsibility to see that we both have proper guidance in the female virtues.

Ladies must surely run, I thought, *if they are escaping from wolves . . . or from a red-Indian man.* But I said nothing, and Jane did not speak of our strange encounter, either. We only looked at each other. Then — we could not stop ourselves — we laughed and laughed.

Our mirth made Mother Rodgers even more cross. "I do not know," she said, "that you girls should be out walking anyway. Just now I heard that strange call again. I care not that they are only birds, as Dr. Rodgers tells me. I like them not at all." And she rose suddenly from the rocking chair, holding Percy tightly against her shoulder, and went to add fuel to the stove. She thrust into the fiery cavern a shovel filled with dried buffalo dung, and added fiercely, "That terrible sound brings me near to weeping."

My stepmother's last words made me go still. Would I

see her weep yet again? I am accustomed to seeing her looking pained — toward me; pleased — toward the littles; compliant — toward Papa; and tired, always tired. I am not accustomed to her weeping.

But she merely drew herself up from the stove and began giving orders. "There is mending that must be done, Polly. And the breakfast dishes to be washed, the floor to be swept. Luther and Cal are already in the garden weeding, and Nellie is to help me again with bread. The yeast we started is more lively now, so the bread should be lighter."

Jane nodded to me and slipped away, back to her life with her papa, a life she no longer speaks about to me, and we had no chance to say whether or not we would meet with the young red-Indian man in the morning.

I know for a certainty, though, that I will go, and I will be most surprised if Jane does not do so, too.

What would Mother Rodgers say if she knew we were going to meet a heathen savage on the morrow? I have heard her call them such, despite all Papa has said.

Of more importance, what would Papa say? He says these native people should be respected, even pitied. He says that as Baptists we can understand better than most what it is like to be downtrodden, so we must needs pity them. But would he approve of this meeting?

It is strange to think about, but that young man saved our lives, and we did not even thank him. We did not so much as ask his name.

SATURDAY, 12 JULY

His name is Ozawamukwah. I can only guess at the spelling. He tells us his name means Red Bear. Ozawa . . . red. Mukwah . . . bear. Jane and I had difficulty remembering and pronouncing a name so unusual to our ears, but we set out to learn it as best we could and came to pronounce Ozawa. I suppose he must find it odd to be called only Red, but he did not say so.

His skin is not red at all, by the way. Rather it is a beautiful chestnut color. And he is clearly no savage, if any of his people be. He has been to an English-speaking school run by missionaries, and he speaks well. I asked what denomination the missionaries were, and he said only "Christian," so perhaps he does not understand the distinction between Baptist or Methodist, Presbyterian or Catholic that is so important to us, and there seemed little point in trying to teach him. I asked instead if he then knows our Lord Jesus, and he made a curious reply. "I have heard the story told," he said.

I asked no more.

He also said, casually, as the three of us walked side by side, that at a time when the government was paying for Indian scalps, many of the scalps delivered for payment of the bounty were those of Indians who had become Christians. Christian scalps were, he said, so much more easily obtained!

I am not sure what this meant, but when he said it, Jane gasped and reached out to touch his arm, then realizing what she had done, jerked her hand back as from hot coals. Ozawa looked down at his arm — he seemed to be looking for some kind of mark her touch might have left — and then at Jane. Then he smiled a radiantly white smile, for he has the handsomest teeth I have ever seen on a man grown.

I am forgetting, though, what I set out to tell.

Ozawa had asked us to return this morning to the place where he found us, and we did so, finding him waiting when we arrived.

"Come," he said, and he led the way to show us what had prompted the howls of the wolves. We found there the remains of a deer the pack had brought down. Just bones, some scraps of hide. We had, he said, been too close to the place of their feasting, so they had howled to warn us away. That was all. If they had wanted to hurt us, they could have pounced on us with angry growls and slashing teeth, but instead they used their voices only.

"Wolves," Ozawa said, "are gentle creatures." And to prove his point, he took us with him perhaps half a mile farther up the river and showed us a hole dug in a small hill that he said was this pack's den. Most of the pack must have been off hunting again, for only one wolf lay near. When Ozawa approached, she rose and moved away, just a short distance, giving him space. Ozawa spoke to the wolf in his own language, and, never taking her golden eyes from his face, she lay down again and put her chin on her paws, apparently satisfied with his explanation of our purpose there. Then he got down on his belly and crawled into the den, leaving Jane and me staring at each other. A short while later he appeared again, wriggling backward this time, and what should he hold in each hand but a tiny wolf pup!

The pups looked like miniature bears, brown bears with bright blue eyes. They blinked in the sunlight and wobbled when he set them on their feet. Jane and I crept forward, observing assiduously the creature who was overseeing den and pups, and each picked up a pup. They were the dearest mites! The one I held even began to suck on my finger the way baby Percy used to do when he was hungry and having to wait for his mothers' attentions.

The wolf who had been left behind to watch did just that . . . she watched. She watched every move that we made, and I did not doubt but that, should she have decided the pups were in danger, we would have met with her sudden wrath. She was, Ozawa pointed out, an older sister who was baby-sitting, not the mother, because she was a yearling, not yet fully fleshed out, and she carried no milk for the babes.

I was embarrassed to have a young man take note of such a point, but he seemed to feel not the slightest awkwardness in saying so.

And then it was time — past time, really — for Jane and me to return home, and we took our leave. But Jane lingered behind for some last words with Ozawa, though she had more reason than I to be concerned about being late. She has told me that her father sometimes grows exceedingly angry when he returns home and does not know her whereabouts. When she joined me, however, she did not tell me of what they spoke, though her face seemed calm in a way I have not seen it for a long time.

I wonder if we will see Ozawa again.

I wonder, too, if either of us will ever tell anyone of this adventure.

It is bad enough for young ladies to be with a man unchaperoned. But to be alone with a heathen savage!

The Lord's Day, 13 July

I love the Lord's Day better than any other. Not, I must confess, for the services we attend, morning and again in the evening. Not for the Bible reading at home, either, though any other day I love to hear Papa's voice when he reads aloud. We hear so much of Papa on the Sabbath, however, that sometimes I must struggle to suppress a yawn when he brings out the Bible to read at home. Not to mention the struggle to keep the littles attentive and quiet.

What I love the Lord's Day for, though, is the work that is put aside. The meals already prepared on Saturday and eaten cold, the clothes unwashed, the packed dirt floor unswept, the garden unweeded.

For we do no work on the Sabbath, though Papa allows us other quiet activities. In Jane's house, Mr. Thompson permits no reading except it be from the Bible. Nor does he permit Jane to write in a journal or tat or draw. If she had a piano, she would be forbidden to play it. He says novels are wicked, too, that they are lies. All such activities take us away from the Lord, Mr. Thompson says, though Mrs. Thompson, when she lived, was never so strict in such matters, and Mr. Thompson took little notice of his children's behavior on the Sabbath then.

But Papa says we can be no closer to God the Creator than when we ourselves create or enjoy another's creation, and so he is well pleased to see Mother Rodgers at her piano or me with my paintbrushes or reading a beloved book. And so this day I took out my watercolors and a small parcel of watercolor paper brought from home.

I have a book on drawing, too, written by John Ruskin, as fine an artist as one could hope to be instructed by. Because I know I shall find no more of either paint or paper in these parts when these I have brought from home are gone, in all these months I had not used the paints I brought with me. Instead, I have often pored over Mr. Ruskin's book and planned what I should begin to draw when the time was right.

Today, for the first time I know what it shall be. I shall paint a scene from home, the rolling hills, a village of stone houses, the trees. Especially the trees.

Of all I long for from home, I most miss the beautiful old trees. Their overarching limbs. Their sweet shade. Their stately demeanor. If I could have only one of the gifts I left behind in England, it would not be a loaf of bakery bread, crisp of crust with no taste of cinders about it; it would not be the schoolhouse where I went each day to learn; it would not be the brick house that encircled our family, with its wood floors and warm carpets and light streaming through great windows. Instead, it would be the trees.

Mr. Ruskin says that to understand the shape of a tree one should hold a hand up before a glass, cupped as though supporting a large bowl, and sketch the hand and its rising fingers. Then he says to turn it palm downward and sketch again to get the action of the lower boughs in cedars and other such spreading trees. And so I have gone out from the dimness of the sod house to the harsh light of the prairie, carrying Mother Rodgers's small mirror, and I have taken a sheet of my precious paper and completed several such sketches.

The next Lord's Day I shall begin the picture itself, rolling landscape, stone houses, trees, especially trees, drawn entirely from my memory.

Is it possible to hold something so grand as a tree in one's heart and then put its likeness down when the time is right? I hope it will be so.

If Jane's father allowed her such a Sabbath pursuit, what would she paint? A brown wolf pup with startlingly blue eyes?

Or perhaps a handsomely burnished face framed with long, dark braids?

Wednesday, 16 July

The sun bears down on us from the sky. What thanks we would give for a good Dorset cloud to cool its face!

We know now what the builder meant when he said our sod house was good in many ways. Its dark interior is, I believe, the coolest place in Clay County.

The Lord's Day, 20 July

This day the congregation held an election as to whether Papa should be called to be their pastor. Despite the mean talk in the course of the election, they voted that he should be so.

"He knew there were no trees in this place," one said. "He had been here to see. Why did he not tell us?"

"He is in the pay of the railroad," another said. "He needs no living from us!"

Another said, "We have already had a taste of what winter will be like in this place. Did he not know?"

And all about us people murmured, murmured with my papa as the subject of their discontent.

Finally, Papa rose and spoke, and I write down his words as best I can.

"Friends," he said, "as to the winters here in Minnesota, I

have heard the excessive cold of the season advanced as an argument against colonization, but let us wait until we can greet the season on our own before we judge it. For I have also been told by some English residents that the winter season is the most enjoyable time of the year.

"Also, as to being the paid agent of the railway company, this is a mistake. When I engaged to organize a colony for their line, they promised to give me as much money for my work as I had been receiving from my congregation in England, and to bring me and my family out free of charge, and my income was to continue a few weeks after my arrival in this country. They paid me all they promised to pay, and up to the day they had promised that my income should be continued, and I have no fault to find with them. They have acted most honorably toward me, but I have not now an income from them."

And finally he said, "It is stated that my representations of this country were false, and it is implied that but for my lies, many of the people would not have come here at all. To this I can only say that I have not intentionally said one untrue word, and I still think that for farmers this is a very fine country. Such will do well here."

And he sat down.

So the talk went on until my head spun, and finally I had

to get up and take the littles outside, for they could sit still no longer after sitting for three hours of the church service, too.

Much time later, when all came streaming from the church, I asked Luther, who had stayed inside, what had transpired.

"Papa has been elected pastor of the congregation," he said, and I rejoiced.

"Have they voted him a salary?" I asked, quite holding my breath.

"Yes," said Luther. "They have voted him $240 a year."

I released my breath in a great flood. No man with a wife and nine children, seven of them still under his roof, could be wealthy on $240 a year, but as has always been the case in England, we would eat. We would have enough to satisfy all our most important needs.

But then Luther added, "Papa refused the salary."

"What?" I asked, completely bewildered.

"He said" — and though Luther sounded angry, I could see that he was as bewildered as I, or perhaps he was frightened, it was hard to tell — "he said he would accept no salary, that he and his family would instead live on what the congregation sees fit to give us each week."

And Luther turned and strode away.

I stood there, the littles gathered around me, Millie

wiping her gummy nose on my skirt, Glad leaning into me as though I were a tree to hold him up, even Laura quiet for a change. I stood there waiting to see Papa come out of the church.

How could he have turned down a salary? He has always had a salary from his congregations. Without such a guarantee, how are we to live?

When Papa came out from the church at last, Mother Rodgers at his side, he stood tall. Papa was smiling, but Mother Rodgers's face held hint of neither pleasure nor ease.

Our lives will depend on the daily goodwill of the people of the congregation, a congregation who seem to have little goodwill toward Papa at all.

I do not doubt but that this thought will awaken me in the dark of the night like a sudden storm . . . or rather as the stillness before the storm. A stillness in which I will lie waiting for the disaster that is sure to strike!

WEDNESDAY, 23 JULY

This day we woke to find a mouse swimming in the water bucket. Mother Rodgers dashed the water out the door, disturbing a toad who sat in the sunny doorway growing fat on bugs.

Luther grumbled when he had to go back to the river for another bucket of water. If he had risen first to meet the mouse, I think he would have helped it out and left the tainted water to us.

Friday, 25 July

This day we witnessed a strange and delightful performance. An old Italian man came singing his way into our barely formed town. He rode in a closed cart pulled by an ox. When many had gathered around, including Mother Rodgers and the littles, Luther and me and Cal and Jane, but not Mr. Thompson, the man climbed down and went to the back of the cart, returning with a great brown bear following closely on an iron chain. The bear, we soon discovered, could dance.

And so the man sang more, "Didy, didy ont didy ont, ont." And the bear raised himself on his haunches and danced in a large ring around the man, who held him fast on the chain. At the end of the dance, the man said, "Kiss me," and the great bear put his paws on the little man's shoulders and put his mouth up to the man's cheek.

People had few coins upon them to pay for this fine performance, but such pennies and nickels as they had were dropped into the man's hat. And when all was finished, the man turned to us and asked, "Tell us, where is your saloon. For Bruin's reward in this is always a pail of beer."

At first all stood still, no one answering, for, of course, no saloon is allowed in Yeovil.

Then Jane said, "But wait," and she hurried away to her house. A moment later she came back with a berrying bucket, sloshing full of a golden liquid that could only have been beer.

"Here you be," she said, putting the drink down before the bear. And the bear did indeed dip his muzzle into the bucket and drink.

Then bear and man climbed back onto the covered cart, and the ox lumbered on.

"Where did you find beer?" I asked Jane later, but she turned away without answering.

Later, Luther, who has always been more wise than I in the ways of the world — not because he has more sense but because he is allowed more freedom to explore and learn — answered me quietly. "Mr. Thompson makes his own beer," he said, "just as Mother and Nellie made the yeast for their bread."

Such news concerns me greatly. If he makes his beer, that must also mean that he drinks it, too, not just when he goes off in search of a blind pig but on any day of the week!

Oh, how I pity my poor Jane. But since she turned from my question, her chin lifted high, I keep my pity to myself.

THE LORD'S DAY, 27 JULY

Back to my drawing. I have begun, at last, to work on the pictures I have held in my mind for so long. First, I have sketched the great old trees. Master Ruskin says, "Always take more pains in trying to draw the boughs of trees that grow *towards* you than those that go off to the sides; anybody can draw the latter, but the foreshortened ones are not so easy."

Such advice, I fear, is less difficult to give than to follow.

Laura hangs on me, watching every stroke of my pencil, asking questions, even offering advice. I know she wants to draw, too, to dip an eager brush into my paints. But these few sheets of paper and my small supply of paints are precious. I had no idea when I packed them how precious they would prove to be. I thought I should be able to buy more when they were used. Since I cannot, I do not mean to share my meager store.

Laura must understand. I cannot share.

MONDAY, 28 JULY

This night I am home alone with the littles. Mother Rodgers and Papa and even Cal and Luther have gone avisiting. Nellie is off with a friend, too. I stayed home because Millie is feeling poorly and could not walk so far. I had but tucked Laura and Glad and Millie into bed and was deciding whether to go to my own bed or to write in this journal when a tapping came at one of the windows.

I went to investigate with a trembling heart only to see what made my heart tremble more. A strange red-Indian man stood outside the window, holding up a gun. I leapt back and ran to pull in the door latch to keep him from entering, but when I returned to the window, he stood there still and once more held up his gun. It was then I remembered Ozawa and his gentle ways, so I held the tallow candle I carried with me up to the window to try to see more. That proved to be exactly what the man wanted, light from my candle, as he desired to repair his gun. So I held the candle to the window with quaking hands, and he worked in its light to fix the thing that was wrong with his weapon.

He then made a motion toward his mouth to say that he was hungry, and I stepped to the door, holding out a loaf of bread. He took it, rubbed his nose on the door casing — a quaint way, I must suppose, to express thanks — and was gone.

I write this entry with an unsteady hand, and yet it is clear that the man meant us no harm.

Is it possible that these "savages" have more need to fear us than we them?

TUESDAY, 29 JULY

We woke this morning to find several dressed rabbits in our doorway. It was only when they were bubbling in an aromatic stew that I told Mother Rodgers about last night's visitor.

The rabbits were, I am certain, from the red-Indian man. Mother Rodgers paused when she knew, but the aroma of the meat already filled our small house, so she could hardly refuse the gift.

WEDNESDAY, 30 JULY

The sun blazes so fiercely in a cloudless sky that I can barely endure it. It seems a different sun entirely than the one that shone in Dorset and Somerset. It scorches the skin and turns brown the plants in the garden, which are just readying to yield their bounty.

We have not had rain for many days. Luther and Cal carry water from the river to pour on our garden, yet the plants still shrivel.

SATURDAY, 2 AUGUST

The story of our red-Indian at the window has traveled through our colony and grown larger and fiercer on its journey. It is now told that the man held up the gun to the window to threaten us, that he took the bread by force.

None speak of the rabbit stew we enjoyed the next day.

THE LORD'S DAY, 3 AUGUST

"This is the day the Lord hath made. Let us rejoice and be glad in it."

I repeated these words Papa had said in church as I retrieved my sketch from last Sabbath and took up my paints. I began with a wash of yellow ochre, the lightest color on the palette of this landscape. My tones will be yellow ochre, raw umber, and sepia. My teacher at home said that darks and lights are like salt and pepper. They draw the eye and give spice to the whole. But the richness is in the middle tones.

Of course, there will be green and touches of cadmium red, too. And blue for the sky. Cobalt blue made pale.

The wash must be laid on quickly on paper dampened with clear water. I work in one direction, laying on horizontal lines, then go back the other direction, being careful never to back over wet paint.

Then I must leave the wash to dry before working on adjacent areas.

Laura watches my every move, and I have to watch her in turn. Millie comes outside with me, too, but she soon runs off to play, having lost interest in my painting. Glad watches, but always from a polite distance, never intruding. But Laura . . . Laura is constantly dipping a finger into my water, picking up a brush, touching the paper when it is not yet dry.

"Your mother is calling you," I say. "It is time for your piano lesson."

But she does not move. She knows that, though Mother Rodgers plays the piano and Laura may come inside and do so, too, if she pleases, there are no lessons on the Sabbath.

Diary, have I said that Laura receives piano lessons from her mother? She does, but I, who am not Mother Rodgers's true daughter, do not.

It is true that I told Mother Rodgers when we were yet all in England that I had no time for such things and did not choose to learn the piano, but one might think she would offer again. I was but a child when I last refused.

Laura spilled my paint water, wetting my skirt and almost wetting the painting itself.

I should like to spank her, but Papa does not permit me to do so. I said to him once that he should abide by the Holy Book when it says, "He that spareth his rod hateth his son" — or daughter, it must mean, too — "but he that loveth him chasteneth him betimes." And Papa replied, very quietly, "Suffer the little children to come unto me, and forbid them not: for of such is the kingdom of God."

Some days, though, I am not sure even Jesus would suffer Laura.

Monday, 4 August

Rain! At last! Not a gentle misting rain such as we have most often in England, but a pounding, howling, banging rain. The kind that soaks everything in an instant, and then goes on soaking and soaking and soaking still.

This fierce country does nothing by halves!

I grow restless, confined to this dark house, though I am careful not to show how I feel, as Mother Rodgers can always find ample work to occupy my hands. No idle-worms, which are said to grow in the fingers of idle girls, here.

WEDNESDAY, 6 AUGUST

Today Laura ran to Papa, complaining of me, and Papa said in his gentle way, "Polly is my daughter, too, you know."

"But not like I am," Laura said, and though I waited long for Papa to contradict her, he said no more.

THE LORD'S DAY, 10 AUGUST

I painted the trees in my picture this day. Two grand old trees leaning in toward each other to frame the village I will yet paint in the background. And there will be children, two tiny children picnicking beneath the larger tree to arrest the eye and give my landscape a center point.

Even the sky, the soft blue of the sky, will be nearly obliterated by the trees' great leafy branches. One will need only a glance to be drawn into their shade.

Laura stood so close today that she bumped my arm when I was doing a bit of fine work on a limb, nearly ruining everything.

I wish Nellie would keep closer watch on the littles, but she has gone off to her bed to weep, as she does at every opportunity, over her fiancé's failure to follow as he promised.

If I were her, I would have given him up by now and set my cap for another — or perhaps for none at all. If she works hard, a woman can surely make her way in this place, even without the aid of a man.

MONDAY, 11 AUGUST

Once more Jane and I saw Ozawa when we were walking today. In fact, I wondered whether he might have been waiting at the side of the river, hoping to see us . . . or rather, hoping to see Jane.

I have not described Jane's appearance in all these pages, but it is fit that I do so now. Her hair is the color of a bright new copper penny. Her face is pale, her eyes a vivid blue, her lashes long and coppery, too. She has a slender waist and a good figure and, I happen to know, a well-turned ankle. So all in all — though perhaps red hair is not thought among our people to be the most desirable shade to possess — she is most pleasant to look upon.

Despite the Englishman's opinion of red hair, it is, I believe, Jane's hair that most draws Ozawa's attention. One can see that is what his eyes rest upon first each time he turns in her direction. And he turns in her direction often.

We walked with him but a short distance before we had to turn back toward home. In that short time, though, he taught us several new words in Ojibwa.

These are the words we began to learn. *Ahneen* is a greeting. *Wabowayan,* blanket.

Ozawa tells us he is not what whites call a blanket Indian, meaning, I suppose, that he wears the clothes of whites, at least in part, rather than wrapping himself in an Ojibwa red blanket with the point hanging down almost to the ground. He has much respect for his people's ways, he says. It is just that, if they are to survive in this new time, they must learn the whites' ways well and choose those that best serve their needs.

Madjigode is a woman's skirt. *Manominigizi* means rice — the kind of rice his people gather from the lakes. It also means this month, which is August, for this is the month when the lake rice is ripe.

He told us, too, that the buffalo bones we find are not the result only of hunting, though he says far too many animals have been killed since whites came onto this land. In this past century, he says, even his people have destroyed their own bounty, killing for the reward paid by the white intruders. But the bones we find in such abundance are not from such killing alone but from a prairie fire that once caught a herd of buffalo, numbered in the thousands, here in this place.

I had a sense, often, that Ozawa spoke only to Jane, but

when I said as much after we had parted company with him, Jane denied heartily that it could be so. Her face flamed, though, her skin was almost as bright as her hair when she was denying my claim about Ozawa's attentions.

Whether he speaks to me or to Jane's coppery hair, Ozawa gives us much to think about.

He plucked a plant that the settlers call fireweed, I had thought, for its red flowers. But it turns out that it is named instead because it is the first plant to spring to life after a fire has swept across this prairie, killing all in its path. We have seen fires often, but always in the distance, so I have not thought to be afraid. Sometimes fires burning on the horizon make a dawn before the sun has appeared.

But this plant Ozawa showed us grows everywhere on the prairie. Everywhere. As the bones lie everywhere, too. Which means we have been foolish not to be afraid.

"Perhaps," I said to Ozawa, "our people should not have come to this place. The land is not kind."

At first Ozawa was silent, and I thought he had not heard my words, but then at last he spoke. "The land is good," he said, "to those who know how to honor it."

And I knew, even as the words dropped from his lips, that we are not people who know how to honor this land.

Wednesday, 13 August

Papa can no longer bear Nellie's weeping. A German man came this day and carried away Mother Rodgers's piano. Papa sold it to acquire the money needed to send Nellie back to her fiancé in England.

It should have been her fiancé sending the money, but such a thing looked never to happen, so Papa found a way to get together the money for her return home.

Mother Rodgers said nothing, though she turned her back so as not to see the men laboring to lift the piano through the door. I do not know whether Papa asked her before selling her piano or no.

I do know I wish I had permitted Mother Rodgers to give me lessons many years ago when she first offered.

It was no widow's piano, either, but a good instrument, well made and pleasing to the ear. It was especially so when Mother Rodgers played it, not so much when Laura was on the stool.

Laura, I think, is glad to see the piano go. Lessons were but a torment to her. I know Mother Rodgers is not glad. In fact, though she stayed immersed in the business of canning green beans from the garden, I suspect strongly that she be exceeding sad, though it would not be fitting, of course, for an adult to show such feelings.

Friday, 15 August

Nellie is gone this day. She has broken the year, left before a year was out from the time of her hiring. Though that is a discreditable thing for a servant to do and one that brings about much loss of character, nonetheless, I suppose she will return to England with tales of her hardship here that will bring her much sympathy. Especially from the fiancé she is certain is waiting still.

I wonder, though, if he should turn out to be a fribbler, or trifler, professing rapture for a woman yet dreading her consent.

We all went to the station with her, the station with the sign that still says Hawley instead of Yeovil, to wait for the eastbound train. Nellie stood in our midst still weeping, whether now from grief or joy was impossible to tell, and I thought, *What good to sell Mother Rodgers's piano? Even returning home seems to have done nothing to dam the flow of Nellie's tears.*

And I thought, too, *Now there will be more space in our bed.*
I am a wicked, selfish girl.

TUESDAY, 19 AUGUST

This day Jane and I went to Chants' store, she with money in her hand to buy some articles for the house, I with empty hands to watch and wonder. Jane bought a dustpan, a toaster, and an eggbeater for 75 cents. To that she added a large dishpan, iron kettle, and bread pan for another $1.60. A coffeepot, two dripping pans, and a cast-iron spider for frying added another $1.45. She ended with two yellow bowls, a flour sifter, and two kettles for $1.

I added all and it came to $4.80 — more money than I have seen in one place since we arrived here.

"You are near a full-grown woman," I said to her, "keeping house so well for your father."

But she only piled her purchases in the pull cart she had brought for the purpose and said naught.

My Jane is slipping away from me. I know it.

MONDAY, 25 AUGUST

Those among us who have come to own cattle leave them to move about, seeking grass, and the wanderers often find our soddy much to their liking. They rub and rub and rub against the corners until each one is made quite round. I wonder that some old cow may not someday rub herself through the wall and tumble inside our house.

There was a beetle in our porridge this morning. Mother Rodgers flicked it out with a spoon and did not even pause in ladling out the bowls.

Our standards change in many ways. At first I saw that Mother Rodgers put on her silk gloves before picking up the dried buffalo and cow chips we use mostly to fuel the stove. We can buy the coal or wood the train brings, but the buffalo and cow chips are free, and gathering them keeps the littles out of mischief. Later I noticed she did not bother with the gloves but washed and washed her hands each time she added fuel. Today I saw her tossing in the chips, wiping her hands on her apron, and proceeding on without pause to cook.

We have, after all, none of us died yet.

Friday, 29 August

For two weeks I have had little time to write to you, dear Diary. I have barely had time on the Sabbath itself to add to my painting, for I have learned to have cause to regret Nellie's leaving. Much of her former work now falls to me. I even tried this day to make the bread, but found I do not have the feel for it in my fingers. Still . . . there is much else for me to do.

How would Mother Rodgers manage if she had not married a man who had a daughter, waiting to do her bidding?

THE LORD'S DAY, 31 AUGUST

This day I have completed one painting. The children in the foreground, tiny but catching the beholder's eye. The stone houses in the distance, set at a three-quarters angle to the sun so they are defined by their shadows. The rolling, tree-dotted land.

I have used an atmospheric style, so that all grows less clear as it moves off into the distance, as happens when our eye looks out across a real landscape.

Most important in my painting, though, are the trees, the grand old trees, which frame everything and give the scene its charm.

I am not through yet with remembering trees, remembering home, so next Sabbath I will begin another drawing. This one, again, of an English countryside. This one, again, to be filled with trees. In fact, I think there shall be no village next time, only trees.

I shall add, perhaps, just off from the center as before, not children this time, but a couple. A man and a woman, just turning toward each other.

The way Ozawa and Jane turn toward each other. Not that their turning, of course, has any meaning.

My Jane has turned sixteen, but still she cannot be ready for such things. And Ozawa is . . . well, he is not of our kind.

Even Papa with his fine words about red-Indians would agree with that.

MONDAY, 1 SEPTEMBER

Despite our inept planting, despite all the damage done by the starlings and the passing Canada geese, Mr. Thompson's wheat stands in the field like living gold. It reaches taller than either Jane's or my head. Soon Mr. Thompson, and all the others who have planted, will be ready to harvest.

The days have been clear and hot, fine for ripening. The farmers say we could use another rain, though, before the time of harvest. Another rain would give even this fine crop a boost.

Those who planted potatoes are turning them up by the bushel. Many, many bushels. Whatever else may happen, we are sure to eat this winter.

Perhaps Papa was right, after all. "Tickle the ground and it will smile a harvest."

THURSDAY, 4 SEPTEMBER

Mother Rodgers at last had enough drippings from our occasional wild meat to make tallow candles, the ones we brought with us all being burned down to stubs. A Mrs. White has shown her how it is done, as candles were another thing we purchased from the stores at home.

We tied twisted cotton rags between two legs of a chair and poured hot fat over them. When the first pouring had cooled and hardened, we poured more. And on and on until we had candles the size we desired. If we had money to buy wicks from the Chants' store — or even candle molds, too — the task would be easier.

I think I shall never again complain about being sent to the store with money in my hand to purchase necessities.

FRIDAY, 5 SEPTEMBER

This morning when Jane and I were walking, she showed me a buffalo ring in the prairie. It is an indentation in the earth made by the circling of the male buffalo, running and running around the tightly assembled herd to protect their cows and calves from threat. They pound so hard, they leave a circular indentation in the earth. Later, flowers and other plants grow more lushly for the pounding of their hooves, the driving of seed and fertilizer into the ground.

I asked her where she had come to know of such a thing, but she only smiled and turned her face away, giving no reply.

Where indeed?

SATURDAY, 6 SEPTEMBER

This day some folks nearby killed a steer. Thus they had a party to share the meat before it might spoil. Every stick of furniture was moved outside, even the stove, so there would be room for all. One man played the fiddle, another the harmonica.

Everyone brought food to add to the celebration: rabbit pie, roast coon, smoked fish, johnnycake made from ground corn, chokecherry jelly and fresh garden beans and squash and currant cakes and cakes of caraway seed.

We played spin the bottle and London Bridge and drop the handkerchief. We played forfeits, too, and the young man and woman who lost must needs do a rabbit's kiss, each one nibbling the end of a straw until their lips would meet.

All were feeling gay, and all stayed until the young ones must be carried home sleeping.

The party was surpassing fine, but it put me in a mind to wonder about this strange country. In England, those who farm live together in villages, going out each day to tend their bit of land. But here, the government requires folks to live on the land they farm in order to prove it, so most live separated by miles.

I hear men boast of the freedom they have here. Freedom from bowing before any master. But in the eyes of their women I see loneliness, much loneliness.

I wonder how long one brief party can serve to fill a cavity of such size.

THE LORD'S DAY, 7 SEPTEMBER

This day I began to sketch a new picture. The first I have laid carefully between two boards and put beneath our bed. Luther says that when he has time, he will frame it for me so it can be hung on the wall.

Papa says it is beautiful, that it reminds him much of home. Even Mother Rodgers smiled when she looked upon it, but then she bit her lip and turned hurriedly away as though her tongue might fall out if it praised my work.

Laura keeps bouncing at my elbow, telling me what I

should be drawing in this new picture. She wants a picture of our house in Stalbridge. I would not think she would even have remembered it.

But I have told her no. This is my picture, and I will draw trees. The trees of my longing.

MONDAY, 8 SEPTEMBER

Today was wash day, a hot day with a sizzling blue sky. Perfect for drying clothes, not so perfect for bending over a scrub board. But then in my mind, no day is perfect for the scrub board. Mother Rodgers had gone inside to prepare the noon meal, and I had just hung the last sheet, the last pair of boys' trousers on the line, when I noticed a cloud lying low in the distance. It stretched along the entire horizon, as far as in one direction as in the other, and I called to Cal and Luther, who were picking tomatoes, to see. They came and stood beside me.

"It is a storm coming," Luther teased. "You had best take all those clothes down again."

Yet I stood, watching. All would be glad enough for rain. I wouldn't even mind so much having to take the clothes down for some cool wet. But there was something strange about that cloud. It was dark — ominous looking — and yet it shimmered, too. As though it captured the light. I stood perfectly still, watching it grow, watching it move toward us with great speed.

"Mother Rodgers," I called, and she emerged from the soddy. "Look!"

And then she, too, stood staring, her face creased with concern. Finally she turned toward me. "Well," she said, "I see the Lord has seen fit to send us rain at last. We must hurry." And she began tugging at one of the sheets, already half dry in the brisk breeze that had been blowing all the morning, off the line.

I reached to take down a shirt, but my eyes remained on the advancing cloud. Brief whirlwinds seem to strike it, pulling parts away, either up toward the sky or down toward the ground, but as quickly as a part of the cloud swirled off, more glittering darkness moved in to take its place. There seemed to be no top or bottom to this cloud as there was no end to it from side to side. And an ominous sound came from it, a deep hum.

Then, in another moment, it was upon us, over us and upon us, and we understood for the first time what we saw. What the Lord had seen fit to send us — on this day before the harvest — was a plague of locusts.

Grasshoppers, folks around here call them. Millions of

them. Billions, even. And suddenly they were falling from the sky, clinging to our hair and our skin and our clothes, staring at us with bulging, googly eyes.

Laura and Millie screamed. Even little Glad cried out. And their mother ordered sharply, "Go into the house. Now!" as she reached for another sheet. I wondered, though, as they ran for the door, if there would be refuge from the grasshoppers even there. The very air seemed to be made up of the enormous brown insects. They were landing on everything, crawling everywhere, and even as I pulled clothes from the line, I could not help myself and began to cry.

As soon as they landed, the brittle sound of their wings beating was replaced by another sound. You could hear them chewing, their mouths opening and closing, their teeth grinding. The sound of thousands of scissors opening and closing as they ate everything in sight.

I pulled a pair of Cal's trousers from the line, sobbing now, and Mother Rodgers said, "Leave it! Let us go inside. They want what is green. They won't hurt our clothes."

And so we went inside, carrying with us hundreds of grasshoppers beneath our skirts, crawling up our petticoats, caught even in our bodices and our sleeves, tangled in our hair. Mother Rodgers pulled my dress and petticoat off. I pulled off hers. The little girls and Glad were crying. Percy had awakened in his cradle and was crying, too, grasshoppers crawling over his tiny face. Luther and Cal stomped insects as they fell from our clothes, crushing them with their bare feet. And then they swept them up and threw them into the glowing coals of the stove.

Only outside, they kept falling, falling. They didn't fly down from the sky, they fell from it like hail. Except hail does its only damage in the falling. The damage these creatures could do had only begun when they struck.

We dressed ourselves again quickly, though none had thought of modesty before, and stood watching through the windows. Mother Rodgers was wrong. The grasshoppers did not want only what was green. They ate our garden surely. They ate — we later found — the flowers that bloomed on our sod roof. They ate the paint from the door and they chewed away the wood in the handle of the hoe until it was too rough to hold. And they ate the clothes from the line.

They stayed until evening, and then, as unexpectedly as they had come, they caught a gathering breeze, rose and rose, and flew away again, blotting out the sun as they went.

When Papa came home — for he had been out visiting — Mother Rodgers spoke harshly. "We are cursed," she said. "God never wanted us to come to this land."

For once, Papa had nothing to say.

I thought of Ozawa and his people, starving because so much of the game had been killed off by and for our people. I thought of the bleached bones that covered the earth everywhere they had not yet been gathered before the plow. I looked at the bleakness of this house, like a cave carved out of the earth, and at the bleakness of the land, stripped of all that could sustain life. I looked at the faces of my two brothers and at the littles, hiccuping sobs. And I looked at my stepmother, her eyes deeply shadowed, her mouth tight to hold back her misery.

And I thought, *She is right. Mother Rodgers is right. We are surely cursed.*

Monday, 29 September

I have not written in these pages for many days. The truth be told, I have not the heart for writing. But today a disaster has befallen me, one more poignant, more personal to me than the destructive raid of grasshoppers. And I find I must write again, for I have no place else where I can safely speak these words.

Papa says we are not to be angry, and I can face, without anger, a land scoured clean of all that sustains us. Who, after all, can be angry with God, who made the grasshoppers? But being angry with Laura is another matter entirely.

Yesterday evening, when I went up into the loft to prepare for sleep, I discovered that Laura had found her way into my watercolors, into my precious paper. She had wet the paints and daubed a bit on this page, a bit on that one, using up much of my paint and every single piece of untouched paper I brought with me from England. She had put a wet brush from one paint to the other so that of the colors that were left, all were mixed and smudged.

She had even allowed her kitten, Pudding, access to paint and paper, and besides her brush marks there were colorful paw prints across each page as well.

I wanted to scream at her. I wanted to strike her. I wanted, at least, to go running to Papa and accuse her. But I did none of those things. I knew that if I had screamed or hit, I should be the villain. And if I ran to Papa he would emerge from his deep dream of next Sunday's sermon only long enough to look disappointed . . . and as I am the older, his disappointment would be directed at me.

So I gathered up the ruined paper and carried it downstairs to the stove. Mother Rodgers saw me put the pages in, and her eyes questioned, but she did not ask, and I did not speak.

Later, I was sorry to have been so rash. Perhaps there would have been paper good enough to use on the other side of Laura's scrawled pictures. Perhaps I might even have found a way to incorporate Laura's childish smudges into a picture of my own design. I was so heartsick, though, when first I saw all my good paper ruined, my paints used up and spoiled, that I could not imagine doing either.

So I now have two completed pictures to remind me of home, and I shall have no more. I still have the pictures that bloom inside my head, of course, but I shall put no more to paper. And there will be no paintings of this place to keep it in my memory . . . only these words on the page. I need naught to remind me of these days, however. All is emblazoned on my heart, a kind of scar.

I shall never paint again. I am certain of that.

FRIDAY, 3 OCTOBER

This day a strange thing happened. A large snake found its way into our soddy and stretched itself out in the middle of the floor. Since Mother Rodgers chose to have a roof of boards, it could not have fallen from above as it might well have in an ordinary sod house, so it must have made its way over the threshold or come through a crack in the wall.

Mother Rodgers gave out a small cry when she saw the snake, quite grandly striped — or was it spotted? All happened so fast after that I am not sure I know any longer what it looked like. The rest of us simply stood staring. A snake in our midst! A snake in our very home!

Mother Rodgers alone was moved to action. She ran outside and returned with the hoe. Her face white, she scooped the hapless fellow up and lifted it across the doorsill on the blade of the hoe. There was something about her manner, though, so composed, so determined, that caused me to follow to see what would happen next. And of course, the littles all followed me.

When Mother Rodgers had stepped through the doorway, she dropped the snake onto the ground in front of the house. Then, without making a sound, without changing her expression in any way, she lifted the hoe and sliced the snake in two before it could slither away.

She then raised the hoe and struck again the two parts of the snake. And again and again and again she struck until I could no longer watch. Still she continued striking.

When she stopped at last, Mother Rodgers drew a deep breath, very carefully propped the hoe once more against the side of the house, and without looking at any of us who stood watching, turned back inside the soddy and resumed her duties as mother and wife.

MONDAY, 6 OCTOBER

A farmer asked what he thought of the joys of farming in Minnesota answered this way: "What do I think of the joys of farming? What do I think of a hen's hind legs? There ain't no such thing!"

I might say the same of the joys of being a settler in Minnesota.

TUESDAY, 7 OCTOBER

I saw Ozawa again today. At least I think it must have been Ozawa I saw. He sat astride a horse, a pretty chestnut mare with white stockings, but he was riding away from me.

What was strange is that another person, a woman or girl, it must have been, sat astride the horse directly in front of him. Because Ozawa's back was to me, though, I could not see who rode with him, but only the blue gingham of her dress.

Jane has a dress of such a blue gingham, but it could not have been Jane I saw. Not sitting astride a horse before a man . . . a red-Indian man!

Such a thing would not be possible!

FRIDAY, 10 OCTOBER

This day we have dug all the potatoes and turnips from our garden. The rutabagas, too. Some call rutabagas Minnesota apples, as they are good and sweet when eaten raw, and as no one has seen an apple tree in this place. We dug carrots and onions as well. Little else was left to us by the grasshoppers except for that which was growing beneath the ground and the beans Mother Rodgers had already canned.

Papa says the grasshoppers are actually Rocky Mountain locusts, but everyone here calls them grasshoppers or simply hoppers. I suppose it does not matter what they are named, they accomplish their destruction still, and this winter, which was supposed to have been a fulsome one, is going to be scant indeed for many. Not all had planted gardens to be left, at least, with that which grew beneath the ground, and the remaining harvest of corn — I mean wheat — is meager.

Mother Rodgers says all we have harvested from our garden must be packed away in a dark, dry place where the temperature does not vary, but since our soddy has no cellar, we have no such place. She has put the vegetables, except for the onions, into barrels, bedding them down in moss, and put those away in a corner of the house.

Some of the turnips grew so large in our virgin soil that it was hard to believe they were turnips. They seemed more like pumpkins. The potatoes, too, were abundant.

We singed the roots of the onions with a hot iron to stop their growing and hung them from the rafters. It does not do to pack potatoes and onions away together, for each will make the other rot. The harvest of root vegetables looks fine. But will it be enough to carry us through the winter?

It must, for wheat for our mush and for bread — Mother Rodgers's bread has greatly improved — shall be scarce. What seed the farmers have managed to save must be used to plant again in the spring. I wonder sometimes, though. Who will remain here in spring to do the new planting?

MONDAY, 13 OCTOBER

Yesterday evening after the sun set, a persistent glow remained on the western horizon. It remained and grew stronger as though the sun would change its mind and climb back over the horizon again.

We all stood outside the soddy, watching, speculating about the cause of the strange red light.

And then it came to us, to Papa and to Luther and me, all in the same moment. *Fire!* The prairie grasses, grown dry in the summer heat, were burning. And still we stood, each one imagining the conflagration approaching us, surrounding us, licking at the grass beneath our feet, sweeping away the last of what we have managed to preserve in this bitter land.

Father stood watching the growing light as though it were some kind of exhibition. But Luther came to himself first and said we must have a fire break, that we must dig trenches and set back fires to burn away the grass close to our house so the larger fire could not take us. He and I and Cal set out to do just that. Even Mother Rodgers helped.

Papa said, "I will go off to warn the rest!" and he left us to it.

We worked until we were all exhausted, plowing three strips around the entire house, burning the grass away between the strips. Finally Luther turned to us and said, "I have heard it said that a soddy is one of the safest places a person can be in a fire." And we all fell, filthy with soot and dirt, into our beds. When Papa came home from delivering his warnings, I do not know.

In the morning when we woke, the fire had not reached us but had burned itself out some distance away.

Papa gave thanks over our breakfast. However, I could not help but think that there were some — be they red-Indians or settlers like us or even the prairie chickens and the small striped squirrels who live in the grass — who were, last night, not held safe by Papa's God.

Wednesday, 15 October

Papa traded an Ojibwa man a pound of sugar for a horse today. He said it was a very good trade, though Mother Rodgers asked him, her voice as close to anger as I have ever heard when she speaks to Papa, how he expected to feed a horse over the approaching winter.

"The Lord will provide," Papa said.

"As He is providing for us?" she countered.

And Papa said, "But He is providing for us, Mrs. Rodgers. Is He not?"

She said no more.

Still, it is exciting to own a horse. Our family was never able to afford a horse in England, and this is a very pretty gray mare.

Thursday, 16 October

Late this day another red-Indian man, one we had never seen before, presented himself in our doorway. Papa was gone visiting, and Luther was off, too — who knows where — so Mother Rodgers and I had to speak to him.

He was a large, powerful-looking man, but he did not push his way in as we have been told some are wont to do. He just stood in our doorway and, with many gestures and a few words, explained that the horse Papa had bought with sugar rightfully belonged to him. The mare had been stolen from him, it seems, by the man who sold it to Papa in exchange for sugar.

Mother Rodgers motioned for the man to wait, and she and I both hurried off to try to find Papa. I went one direction and she the other, and when neither of us found him, we met again, out of breath, a short distance from the soddy.

We returned to the soddy together to discover the man who had come to claim the horse sitting inside our house dandling baby Percy, who had awakened and cried in our absence. Percy was giggling, as babies will, quite enthralled with the man's face paint, with his long braids and his beads.

Mother Rodgers went so pale I thought she might faint. She hurried to the man and snatched the baby away. "Go!" she cried. "I cannot find my husband, but take the horse and go!" The red-Indian understood enough to know he could have his horse, and he left.

I wished I could tell her that she need not fear these people so desperately, but of course, I cannot. She knows nothing about Jane's and my encounters with Ozawa, and she would not have thought well of us if she did. No girls our age of proper breeding consort alone with a young man, not even a properly civilized one.

When Papa returned home finally he told Mother Rodgers that she had done the right thing. But now we are without a horse and shall be low on sugar as well.

All conspires against us in this place.

FRIDAY, 17 OCTOBER

This morning when I awoke and first went outside to relieve myself, I stumbled across a buckskin bag resting on the ground next to the door. Upon examining it, I found it packed full of the golden sugar the Indians make from tapping the maple trees in the land farther east, well more than the pound Papa had given in exchange for the stolen horse.

The red-Indian man who took back his horse must have brought it. Papa says this man was clearly more honorable than many a white man, who might have reclaimed the horse and not thought about the innocent purchaser's loss.

Mother Rodgers keeps sniffing at the sugar, running it through her fingers as though she expects to find something ugly within, but the bag contains only sweet sugar.

SATURDAY, 18 OCTOBER

As it grows more crisp outside, and warm in the soddy because of our stove, we are overrun by mice. They scurry beneath our feet, nestle in the cupboards. One even made a nest in the hood of Laura's cloak.

Mother Rodgers says nothing when she sees one, but her face goes tight, and she runs to fetch a broom. They are quicker than any broom, though, however fierce the swat.

I think they hide in the corners, grinning.

We are, at last, thankful for Laura's kitten, who occupies himself in their pursuit and grows quite fat on his successes.

He is apt to remain fat, though, for the parade of rodents in this earthen home seems quite endless.

MONDAY, 20 OCTOBER

I went to Jane's house this day to seek her out, as I have not seen her these past two weeks. Unless that glimpse I had of blue gingham on Ozawa's horse was Jane, though surely it could not be.

When I arrived there, I heard shouts. It was her father's voice, sounding slurred and garbled as is the way with someone drunk, and no reply from Jane. No reply at all.

I wanted to cry out, to run inside, to take Jane away from there.

I am ashamed to say that I was too frightened to make myself known and turned back home without drawing closer.

I wish I could tell Papa what I heard, but I do not dare do that, either. Not because of my cowardice, but if Jane does not tell even me of her trouble, surely she would be mortified to have it known to others.

Tuesday, 21 October

I returned to Jane's home this day, and though I did not dare walk up to the door, I waited outside for her to appear. She did, at last, carrying a water bucket and heading for the river.

When I caught up with her, she startled as though a stranger had leapt out from behind a tree, but then she smiled her usual sweet smile, and we fell into step, side by side.

"Jane," I said at last when her bucket was full and I could tell from the nervous look about her that she would soon say she must hurry home, "is all right with you?"

"I am well," she said, though she did not meet my eyes as she spoke.

"Your father . . . ," I asked, but could say no more.

"My father is well, too," she said quickly. Too quickly. "He seems to grow more reconciled to life without Mother and Timmy."

Actually I had not set out to ask after her father's welfare. A man who imbibes spirits can hardly be fine anyway. But I did not dare say more.

"Jane," I said at last, after we had walked much of the way back to her house in silence, "will you make a vow with me?"

"A vow?" she asked, turning a puzzled face to me at last.

"Vow that we shall keep no secrets, one from the other," I said. "Vow that all that is important to each of our lives shall be known to the other."

She stopped then and stared at me, her sweet lips trembling.

"All?" she asked. And I could see immediately that she would not take such a vow.

So I spoke quickly, not wanting her to turn away. "If that asks too much," I said, "then vow that if either of us needs help, we will come to fetch the other. Will you make such a vow as that?"

For an instant she seemed uncertain even of those words, but then she nodded. "I will vow that with you," she said.

And so I told her that on the morrow I would bring a nail and we would find a sturdy tree along the river and pound it in. The nail, I said, would stand as an iron symbol of our vow to each other until such time as one of us should draw it out again. It is a custom she knows well.

Again I could see a question in her eyes, but nonetheless she agreed. Then she ducked her head and hurried home, the bucket of water bumping against her legs and splashing her skirts in her haste.

WEDNESDAY, 22 OCTOBER

Today snow is falling. Not the howling, driving flakes we saw when we first arrived, but sweetly falling, sweetly swirling. I walked to Jane's small house through the falling snow, carrying a nail in my pocket. When she came out we walked in silence to the wood along the river. Then I thought to relieve myself of another question I had been carrying as well.

"Do you remember the howling wolves?" I asked.

"Of course," Jane said. She wrapped her shawl more tightly about herself and shivered. "How could I not remember?"

"And Ozawa, who saved us?"

"I remember," she said. There was no shiver this time.

"Do you see him?" I asked. "Has he come back?"

"I have, perhaps, seen him once or twice," she said, but

she turned her face away as she spoke so I knew there was no "perhaps" and that she must have seen him more than "once or twice."

Saying no more, for I had the answer I sought, I took the nail from the pocket of my skirt and chose a tree thicker in trunk than the rest. Jane took up from the bank of the river a rock large enough to use as a hammer, and we took turns driving the nail into the tree. Then we swore, "I will come to you for help should there be need."

When I returned home, I did not know which I felt more strongly. Jealous for the "once or twice" that my dear Jane saw Ozawa without me or fearful for what happens to her when she is alone with her father.

As I snuff the tallow candle and climb into bed with Laura and Millie — and little Glad, who has already made his way over to share our bed — the snow is still falling. I think it will be a long winter.

FRIDAY, 24 OCTOBER

The sun is out and the snow that fell on Wednesday is gone as quickly and gently as it came. Perhaps Papa is right about the winter's being an enjoyable and healthful time of year.

The prairie grass stands tall and golden. The sky is blue

from one horizon to the next. We have potatoes and turnips and onions in our larder. Papa has been right about many things, has he not?

If it were not for thinking about my Jane, my dear Jane, I believe I should be quite happy.

I fear, though, that she will not keep her vow.

TUESDAY, 28 OCTOBER

This day Cal found a gentle bull snake stretched out behind a roll of blankets. His eyes beseeching me to say nothing, he lifted it in his hands and carried it out the door while Mother Rodgers bent over the stove, never noticing that the enemy had invaded her home once more.

FRIDAY, 31 OCTOBER

Tonight is Snap-Apple Night, though some folks called it Crack-Nut Night. Whichever it is called, it is, in England, a night when families sit around the fire and eat apples and crack nuts and tell stories. We had neither apples nor nuts this night, but we had stories aplenty.

Jane came to join us, saying only that her father was away and that she could remain the night, for which I am very glad. It was a fine evening.

Luther told a tale of the giant of Cerne, an enormous and ancient figure of a man drawn into the chalk hills about the town of Cerne Abbas in Dorset. He told how a giant once roamed between Dorchester and the Blackmore Vale, killing and devouring, how, one day, the giant, fatigued from his wicked endeavors, stretched himself out on the hill above the village for a nap in the afternoon sunlight, and how the villagers bested him. They gathered lengths of ships' cable and iron pegs, then streaming up the hill they crisscrossed the cable over his sleeping form and tamped it down until not even a giant's strength could dislodge it. As the giant woke, a shepherd boy stepped up and killed him. The people then dug a trench around his vast form, to remind all of the danger from which they had been spared, and his form remains stretched out on the hill to this day.

I told of the Jack o' Lantern, a fairy light unwary travelers sometimes see in the furze on cloudy nights. When they try to reach the light, thinking it a lantern carried by another traveler or perhaps a candle burning in the window at a friendly cottage, they are led to the edge of a cliff, where they fall to their deaths.

We told of pixies, who leave behind them a dark circle in the grass, a fairy ring, and of stolen church bells that bring the thieves who captured them to their ruin.

Perhaps we told too many stories. I fear the littles shall be waking us all through the night with their dreams. And I sit here writing by the last light of my candle, already having a dream or two of my own. A dream of dear, old England.

GUY FAWKES DAY, 5 NOVEMBER
(MY BIRTHDAY, TOO)

I have always thought it unfair that I should have to share the day of my birth with the day in 1605 when Guy Fawkes was bested in his attempt to blow up Parliament. Perhaps, though, from this time on I shall not care. Papa says, "We are Americans now," and so, though Luther and Calvin begged, we had no bonfire, no stuffed man to be burned. Mother Rodgers said that in any case we had no old clothes that could be spared to make a man.

What old clothes we have we wear since the day the grasshoppers ate our newly washed clothes off the line.

And so Guy Fawkes and all his celebration are over and my birthday is left. I am fifteen years old this day. Though the day went like any other. It might not have been my birthday at all except that Papa spoke a special prayer for me at teatime and little Millie clasped me about the neck in a tight hug.

Not even Jane thought to come to me with some small gift of her own devising.

I think I should go to the woods and pull the nail from the tree, for the vow I'm certain is already broken. Jane needs my help. I know she does. But she does not come to me for that, either.

THE LORD'S DAY, 9 NOVEMBER

Today, Papa discovered from the conversation of some in the congregation after services that a blind pig has sprung up in Clay County, a few miles west of us along the banks of the Buffalo River. It is, I am certain, the place where Mr. Thompson finds his drink.

Papa and Mother Rodgers talked about the new discovery all through the day. They talk of taking a party and destroying the place. If they do, I shall beg to be allowed to come along. They must permit me, as I would take such pleasure in destroying that which is bringing such destruction to my Jane. The snake at our doorway should be nothing to the splinters I would make of that evil place.

THURSDAY, 13 NOVEMBER

Today we did it. Grandmother Chant came with her ox and wagon, and all who joined her piled in or walked alongside, Papa and Mother Rodgers, me, and several other of our neighbors. Jane only blanched when I told her what we were about and would not stir from her house. I told her, though, that every blow I strike will be for her, and she smiled, though her smile was pale. We took with us axes and hammers and crowbars and such tools as each could lay hands upon.

When we arrived, we found a ramshackle place put together with odds of this and ends of that and sealed with tar. I was disappointed, for I had thought to see gilt and mirrors and shelves and shelves of bottles to smash, such as I have heard one can find in the wicked city of Moorhead. In the end, though, we did not care one whit about the looks of the place. We smashed and we tore. We tipped over barrels and cracked them open. We watched the liquid fire that brings such destruction to men pour out upon the ground.

Most of us there, except for Papa, were women and girls, and you never saw women take such pleasure in destruction. One woman said, again and again, "My husband has bought this place. He has paid for every stick that rises from the ground. It is mine to take down." And I thought, over and over again as I battered and splintered all that was before me, "For Jane! For Jane! For Jane!"

On our way back, though, the exuberance soon drained away, replaced with darker thoughts. Such as how little time it would take the place to rise from the ground again. Such as how those same husbands might react when they discovered what their wives had done with their day. But the dark thoughts mattered little. Our task was accomplished, and we were all resolute. We would do it again if need be.

We returned home in grim glory.

P.S. While we were about our smashing, one woman told of having heard of a saloon in Moorhead that has a porch extending out over the Red River. It is said, this woman claims, that when a man grows obstreperous with drink, he is led out onto the porch and there gets a fine surprise. He is dropped through a trapdoor into the river! All laughed on hearing of such a fine comeuppance for an imbiber.

THURSDAY, 20 NOVEMBER

Winter has finally arrived this day. We awoke to low clouds, a dark sky, a harsh wind. And now the snow has begun, flinging itself against the side of the soddy.

It is so dark inside, one can barely see a hand held before one's eyes unless a lantern or a tallow candle is lighted, and we have no abundance either of candles or of oil for the lanterns. At least the stove will keep us warm.

I wonder if we have gathered enough of the dried chips left by all those dead buffalo to carry us through an entire winter. Is it not strange? The beasts are gone, but they warm us still.

THE LORD'S DAY, 23 NOVEMBER

More snow. Papa was unable to hold services in the chapel because the snow is too deep, the wind too fierce for anyone to journey from their homes. No one could go out into this storm and live. And so he held services in this soddy, for his family only, while the wind roared and moaned and the snow piled and piled.

The windows on one side of the house are packed with snow. On the other, they look out as through a thick white curtain.

It seems rather much to be presented with a whole, two-hour sermon when the preacher is one's own papa and there are no others about to hear. I would have thought he would have wished to save all that work and use this week's sermon next Sunday! Surely no one in his family would have complained for missing hearing the results of his long labors just this one week.

WEDNESDAY, 26 NOVEMBER

And still it snows and blows. I wonder about my Jane. How does she fare?

FRIDAY, 28 NOVEMBER

Today a jackrabbit hopped up a drift that rose to the window on the west side of the house and peered in at the plants Mother Rodgers keeps on the wide sill. He was such a pathetic-looking thing with his long ears weighted down with snow that I wished I could have opened the window to give him a nibble. It is just as well I could not. Mother Rodgers would not have been pleased.

THE LORD'S DAY, 30 NOVEMBER

Papa held services this day, but few besides our family made it to the church.

Every time the church door came open, slamming against the wall with the force of the still-blowing wind, I turned back, hoping to see Jane. She never appeared.

Dear Jane, are you well?

Wednesday, 3 December

The sun shines at last, but it shines with a cold fire. The temperature outside is 40 degrees below zero. Inside is not so warm, either. We all wrap up in many layers. But I warrant we are warmer in this sod house with the stove going at the center than in any frame house on all this vast prairie. Not warm, but warmer than most.

Tuesday, 9 December

After days of icy sunshine, the clouds cover us and the snow blows once more. There were but half a dozen people in church Sunday . . . besides our own family. Each person is isolated in his or her own house.

I heard of a man who lost himself between the house and the barn, trying to reach the beasts to feed them. He tunneled through the snow, but missed the barn and tunneled on and on into the prairie. Finally, realizing what had happened, he turned back, but after journeying some distance, digging his way once more through places where the tunnel had collapsed behind him, he came to a spot where he had not the strength to tunnel farther and lay down, the shovel still gripped in his frozen hands, and died.

All these happenings were judged by his family when

they found him, not more than fifteen feet from his own front door, frozen quite stiff.

SATURDAY, 13 DECEMBER

All is strange and different in this new land. It is as though nothing we knew before remains here. For warmth and for cooking we have an iron stove that stands in the middle of the soddy. Being accustomed to open fires in our homes in England, we of course have been keeping the door to the stove open. Our neighbors have, also. And we thought the stove a strange and ineffectual fireplace, for we have been cold every day and growing colder.

This day a Norwegian man stopped by the house, a settler, too, and seeing the open stove, asked why we kept it so. He went over and shut the door, and to our amazement, in a short time, the soddy grew much warmer. He said we have been wasting fuel, keeping it so, as well as suffering cold.

It seems we must learn everything new!

THE LORD'S DAY, 14 DECEMBER

At services this day we heard another tale of woe, though this one amusing, too. One of our families, the Coxes, built a frame house but had not enough money left over for windows, so they stuffed the openings meant to hold glass with hay. They had not money, either, to build a shelter for their ox, and so in these storms the poor beast wanders about outside the house, seeking shelter from the wind.

When the family awakes these cold mornings, they find their house not only cold but windy as well. For through the night, as the ox stands close to the house to shelter from the wind, he avails himself of the ready food and eats their window up!

FRIDAY, 19 DECEMBER

Sun or blowing snow, it hardly matters. With the sunshine comes the bitter cold. With the snow comes a wind strong enough to knock a person over and air so full of flakes that one can barely distinguish up from down.

What did Papa say about winter's being the most enjoyable time of the year? Sitting inside our soddy, I can barely write in my diary, for my fingers grow stiff with cold, the ink freezes in its bottle, and Mother Rodgers will not permit me to burn even a part of a tallow candle to see in this gloom. "They will too soon be gone," she says, "and I have no fat pig or cow to kill to give us more."

Not that she ever killed any animal herself in all her life, but I look sometimes at the cold light in her eye — as cold, almost, as the winter sunshine — and think that she would not hesitate to do so now if one came to hand.

Perhaps I should be grateful that there is not enough fat left on my body to make even one good tallow candle.

TUESDAY, 23 DECEMBER

The littles have got wind that Christmas is almost here, but what Christmas shall be in this place, I cannot imagine.

Millie has asked for a doll with a china head, though I suspect it is Laura who has put her up to the asking. Surely Millie could not remember the existence of such a thing. Glad says he should like to have a pencil and some paper. (How I should like that, too!) Laura surprised me. Perhaps it was Glad's wanting paper that made her think of it, but she asked nothing for herself. Only that St. Nicholas would bring sister Polly more paints and paper for painting. Though I would not wonder that she asks only in hopes of using them up herself

Surely, though, they all must realize that St. Nick cannot reach us in such a place. Not in the midst of all this snow and cold. Perhaps not any place in all this new world.

Remembering home

Christmas at home was always a bright affair. It was the task of the children to decorate the fir tree, held upright in a great tub of sand. We strung cranberries and popcorn and chains of paper flowers, looping the tree round and round with those. We made paper cornucopias, too, filled with sweets and fruit and nuts, one for each person in the family, and hung them high. Dearest of all, though, was the angel atop the tree, with wings of spun glass, a crinkled gold skirt, and a wax face.

I always hated seeing that angel put away again when Christmas time had passed. I wonder where she be now. She must not have made the journey with us or surely Mother Rodgers would bring her out for all to see and remember former Christmases by.

And of course, we always had plum pudding. I remember, still, my mother's recipe for plum pudding, though I might as well dream of angels as dream of having plum pudding in this place. One cannot make such a pudding out of potatoes and turnips and carrots. I remember the making, though.

To make a plum pudding, take of raisins and well-stoned currants, thoroughly washed, one pound each; chop a pound of suet very finely and mix with them; add a quarter of a pound of flour, or bread very finely crumbled, three ounces of sugar, one and a half ounces of grated lemon-peel, a blade of mace, half a small nutmeg, one teaspoonful of ginger, half a dozen eggs well beaten; work it well together, put it into a cloth, tie it firmly, allowing room to swell, and boil not less than five hours. It should not be suffered to stop boiling until it is done.

CHRISTMAS EVE, 24 DECEMBER

No young mother, looking for a stable in which to bear her son, could have survived even a short while should she have been searching here. The sun shines so brightly all the day that the snow, covering the world in its whiteness, blinds any person brave enough to step outside. And yet the cold presses down upon us. And now it is night and the dark, too, presses against our small house like an invisible hand.

We go to bed early, I and all the littles, just to seek warmth. Even Cal comes crawling in beside us. Luther alone stays up, pretending to be a man. He feeds buffalo chips to the stove, but when I peeked over the edge of our loft, I saw him shiver.

No fir tree. No sweets. No doll with a china head. No paper and pencil. No plum pudding. Not even a haunch of venison to roast.

Papa says, "Nonetheless, it will be Christmas. We have the birth of the Christ Child to celebrate in our hearts."

I know I must be grateful for that.

As I huddle down beneath the bedclothes, though, I wonder. Was He born only to die?

Are we all?

I sometimes think that Death may come to all of us in this place, sooner rather than later. And if he comes, will it have been Papa's sin in bringing us here that brings his family — and many others besides us — to such a place?

CHRISTMAS DAY

Mother Rodgers had sorghum for our mush this morning and even a touch of milk.

"Merry Christmas," she said to all, as she served it out. "Merry Christmas."

Only Papa responded with vigor, too much vigor, I could not help but feel, and even he grew quiet after a time.

Cal is more quiet than all. Is it possible that he is growing ill again? If he is, what shall we do for a physician?

There were small gifts, too. Corn-husk dolls for Millie and Laura. For Glad a piece of chalk and a slate. For baby Percy a ball crocheted out of string. For Cal and Luther, new flannel shirts. (I had seen Mother Rodgers stitching on them in the evenings, though of course they, being boys, never noticed what she had in her hands.) For me a pretty apron.

Mother Rodgers said softly, as I opened it, "I wish it could be more paints and fine paper, daughter," and I nearly wept. Not for the disappointment, but for the word "daughter" and for the surprise that she knew exactly what my heart desired, though I had never spoken of my loss.

In the afternoon, when the sun was low, three wolves came and circled our house, stepping on top of the drifted snow. They paused now and then to peer into our windows. Even I, who had once held one of their pups in my hands, shivered before their yellow gaze. Luther said, "I wish I had me a gun."

"Oh, please," I cried out. "You would not kill them."

And Papa agreed. "Surely there is place," he said, "even for such as these on the Christ Child's day."

Luther muttered about the $5 bounty he could get from the government for each wolf, for the added $1.50 he could obtain by selling their skins. But I think, were a gun at hand, he would have no heart for facing those yellow eyes on the other side of that glass anyway.

I could not help but think of the bounty the government once paid for the scalps of our red brothers and sisters. Do they pay it still? And is it yet those who have come to love our Lord who are most often delivered up?

Perhaps these wolves, too, are Christians, though I know it is wicked of me to say so.

I went to bed worrying about Cal. He says his throat hurts him, and I am certain that he has a fever.

SATURDAY, 27 DECEMBER

There is no question but that our dear Cal is ill, and now Laura grows pale and listless, too. It is, I do believe, a quinzy throat they both have.

Grandmother Chant has come to minister to them, but they do not rise from their pallets near the stove.

Mother Rodgers hovers as much, I must admit, over Cal as over her own Laura. Papa paces, though what good he shall do by stomping up and down before his sick children I do not know.

Unless worry be a form of prayer?

Mother Rodgers finally turned on him and said, "Go! Go and fetch a physician. Your children are in need!"

At first I saw from Papa's face that he wanted to ask where he should find such a person, but he did not. He wrapped himself up in his coat and scarf and went out into the flying snow.

Thursday, 1 January

This is a new year. 1874. But no one in this house cares. We care only for the two children, their throats now vividly red, swollen, covered with pockets of white puss. Their breaths rattle horribly.

They burn with fever and Grandmother Chant's remedies seem to have no effect.

The physician does not come.

Friday, 2 January

Still no physician, not even a surgeon, who might be of lesser help, though Papa sent word on the train for the doctor in Moorhead to come to us. Moorhead is the larger city west of us on the railroad. The doctor has only to take the next train east, get off at the Hawley stop, and walk the short distance to our soddy.

Finally, I could not bear to wait any longer. I threw on a cloak and ran out myself, though where I was running to I could not have said. I ended up going to the only place I know . . . to tell Jane of our trouble. It was my good fortune that her father was not in the house.

Jane heard me with solemn face. Then she said, "Wait," and went to a cupboard and drew out a small leather bag.

She brought it to me, saying, "This is swamp root. It is called *jeebkas*. Boil it and have Laura and Cal sip it as often as they can through the day."

I stood with the leather bag in my hand, a hundred questions pulsing in my brain. A thousand. What good could swamp root possibly do our sick children? I had never heard of such a remedy. And what could Jane know of remedies anyway? I had been foolish to come to her, as she has no special knowledge of medicine. If her mother had had any such knowledge to teach her, might be she would not have lost so many babies. Besides, Grandmother Chant, who knows more about healing than most physicians, had already tried every remedy she knows. I had come to Jane only for comfort, because I was afraid.

Still, I returned home with the leather bag in my hand, wondering how I would explain to Mother Rodgers what I had.

As I knew would happen when I tried to tell Mother Rodgers about the swamp root, she said, "Who? Jane Thompson? And what does she know of remedies, pray tell?"

When I could not answer, I thought Mother Rodgers might throw the swamp root away, but she did not. What was the other word Jane called it? Jeebkas? Mother Rodgers stood there for some time, sniffing the contents of the leather bag, looking to the feverish children, sniffing again.

Then finally she said to me, almost crossly, "Set the teakettle to boil. We shall see what good this will do."

And so the children have been sipping, and all have been waiting to see.

I go to bed still waiting.

THE LORD'S DAY, 4 JANUARY

Whatever jeebkas may be, it works. Laura and Cal grow stronger every day.

Papa said I was to stay home from services this morning to watch over them, though I had hoped to see Jane in church and to thank her.

Surely Papa and Mother Rodgers will remember to give her our thanks.

I wonder, though. Will they also ask what jeebkas may be and where she learned of such a plant?

And will she tell them?

WEDNESDAY, 28 JANUARY

Again, it has been long since I have written. The days are so cold without and so dark within, the sound of the wind and the sight of the flying snow so endless. Tallow candles grow scarce. The frost makes intricate designs on the windows: spiked cacti, feathered ferns, marsh pitcher plants.

Last night, in the middle of the night, I awoke suddenly. Millie and Laura woke, too, grasping me on each side and asking, "What is it, Polly? What is it?" But I did not know.

We lay there, all of three of us, trembling in our bed, until finally I knew what it was we had "heard."

The wind had stopped blowing. Simply stopped, like a candle blown out.

Silence lay upon us all like the grip of Death.

TUESDAY, 3 FEBRUARY

I have not said in these pages that Laura and Cal have survived their illness. Neither is entirely well, still. They cough, often, and their faces are thin and pale. But their quinzy throats and fevers are a thing of the past.

Was it Jane's strange medicine that brought them through? It must have been, but so many questions remain.

THE LORD'S DAY, 8 FEBRUARY

We struggled to chapel this morning, pushing our way through snow that reached nearly to our waists. The sky was heavy, leaden, but only a few small flakes whirled in the air. The air was so cold, the fine hairs in our nostrils froze at the first breath. Mother Rodgers kept baby Percy wrapped in her shawl, tight against her breast, yet he cried.

When time came for the services to begin, it was clear that few others would make the journey that day. The church itself was cold, too. I think we were all surprised — and grateful — when Papa kept the service short. We were out and struggling toward home again in little more than an hour.

This time Papa did not say, as he so often does, that he prefers the fierce but invigorating cold of Minnesota to the gray damp of England, and I was glad.

'Twas a good thing the service was so brief, for before we could partake of the soup Mother Rodgers had kept simmering on the back of the stove, the wind was howling again, the snow flinging itself so hard against the northwest side of the house that those windows were immediately covered as if with heavy white paper.

I wish it were paper. If it were, I should face the gale to go out and gather it in. For now it is no longer only drawing paper I miss. I know not what I will do when I come to the end of this small book.

Remembering home

The days were often gray in England, and a damp chill could settle over the land, sometimes even in summer — a chill that penetrated every comer in our house, every bone in our bodies. I remember that.

But I remember, too, when the sun rose cheerfully in the sky and the rolling fields stretched away on every side, radiant with grass, festive with sheep. And I remember the winter snows. They fell so gently, gathered so sweetly in the still-green grass.

No hordes of locusts swept across that land, no fires. The sun never blazed until the grass itself was scorched. The wind never blew until all bowed before it. The snow never obliterated the land, only decorated it.

Papa brought us here. Us and many others.

Many days we cannot go out, could not push past the wall of snow outside the door if we had need, and Papa sits at his writing desk hour after hour. He does not pick up his quill, though, and he does not write.

I wonder what it is he thinks. Does he, too, remember England in this "most enjoyable time of the year"?

WEDNESDAY, 18 FEBRUARY

Two bright sun dogs rose with the sun this morning, rose and stayed with it all the day.

Papa says this is a most enlightened land to sport three suns, but not one gave off any heat.

Luther calls them sun devils, and I would not be surprised but that the devil is in this winter sky as he surely is in this frigid land. Those who speak of the fires of hell are, I suspect, entirely wrong. Hell is not the heat of fire, but rather a place of unremitting cold . . . like winter in Minnesota!

TUESDAY, 24 FEBRUARY

Whereas we began the winter with an abundance of root vegetables, now we reach to the bottom of the barrel to gather a few for each meal, and those withered. We have long since used up the last of our wheat flour. Our meals are scant, and the faces of the littles grow gaunt. Even Papa with his barrel chest seems thin these days. Thin and troubled.

The train has not been through for many days, so even the shelves in the Chants' store grow bare. Sometimes though, Grandmother Chant manages to bring some small food from their store. What Mother Rodgers pays with — or if she pays at all — I do not know.

I know only that the plates passed in church these Sundays have come back mostly as they went out — empty. And Papa without a guaranteed salary.

I know, too, that there is much talk of depression in this land. The railroad that brought us here has gone bankrupt. There is no money to be had anywhere. Cordwood and rat skins are legal tender at Chants' store, though what they want with rat skins I cannot imagine. I suppose the government pays a bounty on the pests.

I asked Luther how we would live to the end of the winter, but he does not know, either. I cannot think why I supposed he would.

SATURDAY, 28 FEBRUARY

It is said that the Northern Pacific Railroad strung nine engines together and used them to blast through the snow piled on the tracks. As many men are hired as the railroad can find to dig away the snow on the tracks, but, of course, Papa does not go out with the rest. No one expects God's minister to do such work, least of all his family.

The store has food again today. The store has food, but what must we use for money?

If Mother Rodgers were not Emily Chant, the

storekeepers' daughter, I wonder that we might not starve entirely.

WEDNESDAY, 4 MARCH

Snow. Snow. Only more snow.
There is nothing more to say.

TUESDAY, 10 MARCH

Word came back this day of a father and a nine-year-old son who set out to bring home their cattle, the father walking, the boy on a horse. A storm overtook them, and the father lay down, wrapping the boy in his coat and causing the horse to lie down beside them.

The two of them, father and son, talked and prayed through the fury of the storm. They talked about perishing and prayed for salvation. The next day searchers found the boy, still wrapped in his father's frozen arms, next to the frozen horse.

The boy lives, but what can be said of such a life?

SATURDAY, 14 MARCH

This day, if the experience of our senses can be trusted, the back of winter is finally broken. The sun not only shines, but actually gives out warmth. Snowdrifts that have built up against every upright object begin slowly to sink back down again, taking on new and strange shapes.

Even mud appears in places. Wonderful mud!

And juncos. I heard Grandmother Chant say that she has been told the gathering of the juncos is a sure sign of spring.

Papa says all will be well this spring. We will plant a garden, the farmers will plant crops, and what we plant will grow, and all will prosper. He goes about whistling and patting the littles on the head. He does not pat Mother Rodgers, though. I suspect her look might wither his hand if he tried.

He does not pat me, either.

MONDAY, 23 MARCH

We heard today of a man who had a 75-pound pig in a small, three-cornered pen. The first winter storm set in so swiftly that the man had time only to put a door over the top of the pen to protect the pig. Next morning, the snow was so deep he could not reach the pig but put down a two-foot length of stovepipe and dropped feed through it. This he continued to do through the winter, adding more pipe as needed.

When the spring thaw came and he could, at last, remove the door and reach his pig, he found himself the owner of a 400-pound sow!

Thursday, 26 March

I saw Jane today. The first time in many weeks. She is thin. That is not so great a concern, as I suppose we are all thin this spring. There is something more, though, something harder to describe than the shadows cast by the bones in her cheeks. Some light has gone out from her eyes. Some light. Some hope.

I mean to go back to the tree where we pounded the nail of our vowing and draw it out. For I know she does not keep her promise.

She needs me. I can see clearly that she needs me. And she says nothing. Nothing at all.

The Lord's Day, 29 March

The geese have returned this day. They made such a commotion, they came near to drowning out Papa's sermon.

I suspect, however, that many sat listening to their braying with as much sense of God's goodness as any sermon could bring.

Monday, 30 March

The melt continues. All runs with water, and mud everywhere is so deep that I have left off wearing shoes. The ground is cold still, but any step can find your foot in mud up to the ankle, and I cannot see my shoes ruined, or even left behind in a slough.

The river that flowed past our small community so gently all this past summer now roars past filled with foaming debris.

The prairie chickens boom in the grass. Boom-ka-ka-boom. Boom-ka-ka-boom. And frogs call everywhere. With every step a frog, long and green, will leap out of one's path. I do not like to see them nearly so much as to hear them, though.

April Fool

Last year this time Timmy had just died, had just been buried at sea. I wish to go to Jane, to hold her in my arms, to weep with her, but something keeps me away.

Somehow I cannot but fear that she would not welcome me.

In the midst of dinner, eating the porridge made from the wheat Mother Rodgers received from the store, Laura said, "Polly, you have butter on your nose."

My foolish hand flew to cover my face, though it has been long since my nose — or any nose in this family — saw butter.

"April Fool!" Laura cried, and all the littles echoed, "April Fool! April Fool!"

I had to smile.

Thursday, 16 April

The strangest thing! Jane appeared at our house this evening, her eyes a little wild, her coppery hair disheveled. Mother Rodgers tried to get her to come in, to take a meal with us — such as our meals be these days — but she would not. She would speak only with me and that must be outside, beyond the hearing of every ear.

"Please," she said after we had gone aside, "remember our vow?"

Remember it! Of course, I remembered it. She was the one who had not! But I said none of this. I told her only that I did and waited for her to tell me how I might be of service.

"If you have taken a vow with your dearest friend," she said, her eyes still alight with something that was almost a fever, "and you have agreed to tell each other whenever you need help, does that mean that you have also agreed to give whatever help might be needed?"

"Of course," I told her. And I promised there was no help I would not give her. So now she must tell me what was wrong.

She would not, though. She told me only that on the morrow "we must go together to the reservation, to the White Earth Reservation." She said it as simply, with as little inflection, as if she were telling me that on the morrow we must go for our usual walk along the river.

"How will we reach such a faraway place?" I asked, utterly bewildered. "And what shall we do once we arrive?"

The latter she did not answer, explaining only that on the morrow she had the use of her father's horse and that she and I would ride together to the reservation.

I stared, knowing not how to answer such a request, but she asked impatiently, "Will you go with me? I must know if you will go."

Dear Diary, what could I say but yes? If I had said no, would that have kept her here?

Tonight I go to my bed filled with trepidation. Two young women riding alone into an Indian reservation?

Surely we will be scalped. Perhaps worse.

I cannot bear even to think about it. But what else can I do? I once made a vow with Jane, an iron vow, and I never did go draw that nail out of the tree. So I must.

FRIDAY, 17 APRIL

This morning I told Mother Rodgers that Jane must have my help and that I would go to her for the day — which is surely the gospel truth — and almost before she had a chance to think *yea* or *nay*, I was off.

I met Jane along the river as she had told me. She had her father's horse with her, a gentle black gelding, recently purchased.

"Now," say I, "you must tell me what you seek."

"Ozawa," she replied. "I seek Ozawamukwah. He be the only one."

Her face was so pale, her eyes so reddened from what must have been long weeping, her head with its bush of flame-colored hair so bowed that I did not dare ask, "The only one *what*?" though surely I wanted to.

Instead I mounted the horse behind her — both of us astride as no lady would dream of riding in England — and we started off, traveling north and east, first along the Buffalo River, then leaving it and moving on without the river as a guide. I was glad Jane knew which direction to go, for I would have had no idea how to seek out the reservation where Ozawa and his people live. Nor would I have thought of doing so.

We rode on in silence. I saw the tiny squirrels called gophers scurrying through the grass. I heard prairie chickens boom. Once a coyote appeared on the top of a rise, silhouetted against the too-blue sky, but I commented on none of it, for Jane seemed in so deep a reverie that I suspected my voice would not be heard.

We came at last to what Jane sought. A group of wigwams rose out of the grass ahead of us, the round homes made by the Ojibwa, constructed of willow branches and birch bark. When we drew close, close enough to see people, a woman hoeing a garden, small children and a great many dogs running about, Jane brought the horse to a halt and slid to the ground, taking the small bundle she had brought with her.

"I will go on alone from here," she said, looking up into my face. "When you reach home again, please return Midnight" — for that is the name of her father's horse — "to my father. I will not have him say that his only daughter stole from him."

I was so astonished that at first I could find no voice, but finally I said, "Dear Jane, you cannot mean to stay. Not here. Not among these —" I broke off, remembering Papa's disdain for the word.

But she supplied it for me. "Savages?" she said. "There are many savages on this earth, Polly. Perhaps there may be some, too, in the Ojibwa nation, but I have not yet known them." And she turned away.

"Jane!" I cried, and she paused, turning back to look once more in my direction. For an instant, I thought surely she would realize the foolishness of her intent and return to me. But she did not.

She said only, "You are a good friend, Polly. My dearest and most cherished friend. I will remember your help this day."

And again she turned away, walking with determined strides toward the wigwams and the people gathered there, all of whom seemed to have stopped now to witness Jane's approach. Even the children stood perfectly still, watching.

I sat on the horse, watching, too. What else could I do? Until I saw a young man striding toward her. Ozawa? Ozawamukwah?

Jane ran to him, and together they made their way toward the watching people. For my part, I could no longer bear to see and turned the horse's head toward home.

It was a long and lonely ride back. When I came near Jane's house, I dismounted stiffly — oh, so stiffly — and gave Midnight a slap to send him the rest of the way to his own abode. I had no desire to see or to speak to Jane's father.

I had no desire to speak to anyone in my own family, either, and went right to my bed — and to this diary — after a silent and meager supper.

Jane. My dear Jane. What will become of you in such a place among such people?

SATURDAY, 18 APRIL

More strange things happening! I have hardly had time since I woke to think of Jane or to wonder what must become of her among Ozawamukwah's people. For we have had proof this day that this land we came to with such exalted hopes is truly cursed.

We had thought the grasshoppers gone, moved on to plague other poor settlers trying to wrest a living from this unforgiving ground. And of course, they did move on last summer. After they had stripped our land bare, they rode a fresh wind on east. But while they were with us, eating the food meant for our sustenance, eating the paint off doors and the wood of our hoe handles and the clothing we had hung out to dry, they performed another chore we barely noticed. They laid their eggs. Millions and millions of eggs. About an inch below the surface of the ground. And not even the deep cold of the winter has disturbed them in all this time.

So on this day the young grasshoppers began crawling from the earth to greet us. On this day the chewing of those hungry jaws began all over again.

These infant grasshoppers do not even fly, and they will not be able to do so for many weeks, so they cannot leave us yet no matter how the wind blows. And in these weeks of waiting for their wings, any green thing that dares poke its head above the surface of the soil will be consumed. Instantly.

I look at Papa, and even his face is ashen.

Some men have come to him — Mr. Thompson, thank the Lord, is not among them, so I have not been required to answer any questions about Jane — and asked that the community hold a meeting tomorrow after services.

At least that means that most will come to services. Perhaps for this time the collection plate will hold enough to buy us some potatoes. Our own barrel is almost bare.

Or perhaps it will hold nothing at all as everyone faces disaster anew.

The Lord's Day, 19 April

The community held a meeting after services, and such a meeting it was. It did not take long for the talk to turn, once more, to Papa, to the people's dissatisfaction with his having brought us all here.

He knew — he must have known, it was said — of the hardships of this harsh land. But for his lies, we would all be safe in England still, not facing starvation here. And more and more.

I sat listening. We all did. Luther, Cal, Mother Rodgers. Even the littles seemed, this time, to take note of the angry words. At least they knew that something was very wrong, and they knew the something wrong had to do with their papa.

Worse, though, I sat and listened and silently agreed with all they said. It is my papa's fault. All . . . all is because of him. The town that did not exist. Even Victoria Park and Albert Square. The treeless land. The snow and cold and bitter winds. The grasshoppers. The prairie that bursts into flame seemingly of its own will. The children whose faces grow daily more pinched and gray.

Even Jane. My poor, dear Jane. That she had nowhere to go to escape her father's drunkenness except to a red-Indian reservation is my father's fault, too. If we had all remained in England, her brother and her mother might yet be living. If we had all remained in England . . .

Finally, I could bear no more, and I rose and left the church and made my way toward home alone without even my dear friend to comfort me.

Dear Jane. What are you doing? What could you possibly be doing among those strange people? When will you return to your home?

And why is it that your father has not once come asking for you?

Tuesday, 21 April

I should not have wondered about Mr. Thompson, because this day he has appeared, drunk, on our doorstep, not just asking for Jane but shouting for her, bellowing for her, roaring her name.

Several other men of the community came with him, none in much better condition than he was, all ready to blame Papa for Jane's disappearance. If a dragon were to descend suddenly from the sky, I am sure they would blame Papa for that, too.

When Papa appeared, Mr. Thompson cried, "You have stolen my daughter away, as you have stolen my wife and my son. You! You!" And he poked a finger repeatedly into the center of Papa's chest as though to stub himself a hole and find his daughter therein.

"I know nothing of your daughter's whereabouts," Papa said in his quiet way.

But Mr. Thompson only roared louder. "But your daughter knows. She was seen going off with my Jane and returning on my horse alone. If you do not know, Polly does. Just ask her."

And then, of course, Papa called me to him and asked me if what Mr. Thompson said were true.

I am sorry, Jane. I am truly, truly sorry. But however much I wanted to protect your secret, I could not lie to my papa.

There was much talk after I told, much muttering and whispering, more shouting from Mr. Thompson, and at last it was agreed that on the morrow Papa and I will be lent two horses, and I will take Papa to show him where I last saw Jane. At first Mr. Thompson wanted to go, too, but Papa convinced him that he would do best to wait at home.

"I will not fail," Papa promised, "to deliver your daughter into your hands."

Will you ever forgive me, Jane, for betraying you? Or is it possible you are already wishing to return home, recognizing your mistake and waiting for us to come?

WEDNESDAY, 22 APRIL

This day Papa and I made the long trek north to the White Earth Reservation. Again for me, for the first time for Papa. We followed the Buffalo River east and north and then moved on across the prairie, following the booming of the prairie chickens, the scampering gophers, the flowers blooming in the grass. At last, we arrived at the reservation. We came to the gathered wigwams, to the people working quietly, to the children running and playing, dogs dancing and barking. And before we had even entered the village word must have passed to Ozawamukwah that we approached, for he came walking to the edge of the village to greet us.

I had thought he might hide from us, but he did not. Instead, he greeted us very politely.

"I am pleased to see you," he said, though surely that was not so. And without another word, we dismounted, and he took us to the mouth of one of the wigwams, went inside, and brought Jane out to us.

How dismayed I was at her appearance! Papa must have been, too. Not because she seemed poorly treated. She looked happier than I had seen her for many months. But because she had put aside the clothes of a white woman and wore instead a dress of soft buckskin covered with beadwork, a dress such as would be suitable for a dark-haired, dark-skinned Ojibwa maiden. Even her fiery hair was plaited in two long braids. She was very beautiful, but she was not the Jane we knew.

Jane threw her arms about my neck, and I hugged her, too. "Jane," I said. "Jane. You must come home with us. Your father pleads for you."

But the instant I spoke of coming home, of her father, Jane drew away from me, her expression changing from joy to one of fierce determination. "I will never return," she said. "No one can require me to return to my father." And she took another step back until she was entirely free of the circle of my arms.

Papa pleaded with her, too, but she would hear none of it.

"I belong here," she said at last, reaching for Ozawamukwah's hand, "with my husband."

I covered my mouth with my hand to keep from sobbing

aloud. She had taken this man, this red-Indian man, to be her husband? How could such a thing be?

"What kind of a life can you have here?" Papa pleaded. "The life these people live is hard. Very hard. And it can only grow more difficult as new settlers flood these prairies." And he reached out to take hold of her to draw her to us.

But Jane pulled away and stood, instead, by the man she called husband. "I will not go," she said. Only that. And she lifted her delicate chin in a stubborn way that was entirely new for my dear friend.

Papa looked sorrowful, but he shook his head, and I knew he was about to insist. I knew, too, that whatever had changed in the few days Jane had been with Ozawamukwah, she would not be able to stand against the insistence of her minister.

"Jane," Papa said, his voice low but filled with the authority of his station. "Jane, you must —"

But Jane — the new Jane — held up a hand to stay my father's words, and then she did a curious thing. She reached up to open the back of her beautiful buckskin dress and then turned slowly until we could see what lay exposed there. Even I, who half knew — would have known wholly if I had ever allowed myself — cried out at what I saw.

Jane's back, her beautiful back, was covered with scars,

some healed, some only beginning to heal, scars from the many beatings she had received at her father's hands.

For a long moment, Papa stood and stared, his hands falling helpless at his sides. Then he went to her and closed the dress very tenderly over the terrible tale told there. "If you come home with us, daughter," he said, "I will protect you. I promise."

"You cannot," she replied. "My father would yet claim me. And even if you could, my home is now here, with Ozawamukwah."

"But —" my father said, and her eyes going suddenly fierce, she interrupted.

"Do you think he would take me back — he and all the fine community of Yeovil — if they knew that I have given myself to one they call a heathen savage?" And she lifted the dark hand that encircled her own and held it before us as though to force us to see.

Papa had no answer to that. Nor did I. A young woman who gave herself voluntarily to a red-Indian man . . . She was right. What place could there yet be for her in a good Christian community?

Papa pleaded still, but the heart had gone out of his pleading. As it had gone out of me. Jane had needed help. She had needed it more terribly than I had ever dreamed. And when she had come to me finally, it was only to be escorted to one who could truly take her away from the horror she had been living.

Perhaps she had been right to do so. What could I have done in the face of her drunken father? What could Papa do now? Even in this country, where the word "freedom" falls so readily from every man's tongue, what freedom is there for a daughter from her own father? Mr. Thompson had only to demand that Jane be returned to his house, and my father would have been forced to comply.

Papa fell silent, standing for a long time with his head bowed, as though in prayer, but when finally he faced Jane again, he said only, "Will you at least allow me to join the two of you before the Lord in a Christian ceremony?"

They both agreed, and right there, with the children and dogs circling, with the men and women gathered to stare, with Jane and Ozawamukwah casting sheep's eyes on each other like any other lovesick couple, Papa performed a wedding ceremony.

When all was finished, Jane took my hand and pulled me aside. "Do not weep for me, dearest friend," she said, for my eyes were streaming. "This husband I have chosen is a good man."

"Will you be happy here?" I asked, gazing at the strange bark dwellings, at the women in their buckskin dresses, at the young children running about without any dress at all.

Jane smiled, and her smile seemed to come from a place much older than any I had yet traveled to. "No life comes with a guarantee of happiness," she said. "And I know I have much yet to learn about Ozawamukwah and his ways. But I can tell you that these past days have been good, better than any I have known since you and I were schoolgirls together in England. And I am certain that more good lies ahead."

I stepped into her arms then. Jane held me long and hard, and I held her. Then slowly, reluctantly, I turned back to my waiting father.

Through all the long ride back, Papa was silent. It was only when the scattered houses of Yeovil, still named Hawley on the railway station sign, came into view that he spoke, at last.

"The people of our community will not be happy with what I have done this day, daughter," he said.

And for the first time in a long, long time, I knew my papa was right. Exactly right.

THURSDAY, 23 APRIL

Before the sun was up this morning, Mr. Thompson stood at our door. He had several others with him once more, as though he knew in advance that his daughter would not come with him except by force.

Papa explained all to the men. He told them of Jane's choice. He told them of the wedding ceremony that left the two married in the eyes of God. But he never once told Mr. Thompson — or those waiting with him — what message we had read in Jane's tender back.

"I will go to that stinking reservation and take her by force," Mr. Thompson bellowed.

"I would not advise that," my father said. "The people whom she has accepted as family would never allow you to take her."

Mr. Thompson raved some more, his words almost without meaning, and Papa said at last, speaking sharply, "She will not come home, man. You alone know why she will never return to you. You must put the matter aside."

At that Mr. Thompson, knowing the truth of Papa's words, turned from our door and went howling across the prairie, flailing his arms, stomping on the young grasshoppers, swearing vengeance against my father and all his progeny.

The men who had come with him turned away, too, their disgust plain for all to see. But their disgust was not with Mr. Thompson, as it should have been. It was with Papa.

"Papa," I said, after all were gone, "why did you not speak of Jane's reason for leaving her father's house?"

But he only smiled sadly. "I find most folks will believe

what they choose," he said, "no matter what reasons are given. And there is no one left for Mr. Thompson to hurt. What could be gained by impugning the man's honor before his fellows?"

And he turned back inside our sod home.

SUNDAY, 26 APRIL

I will not call this the Lord's Day, because what transpired this day has naught to do with the Lord.

The congregation met and took a vote. They voted that the Reverend Dr. George Rodgers no longer be their pastor.

We may remain in Hawley if we choose — even those who came over from England are beginning to capitulate and call it Hawley instead of Yeovil — but if this congregation survives the latest disaster of grasshoppers, they will seek a new pastor for their church.

Papa walked home, surrounded by his family, without speaking. He ate no dinner, but sat with the Bible in his lap, the beautiful Bible given to him by his congregation in England. It has a metal clasp and gilt-trimmed pages, and the births of all in our family are recorded therein.

Through the long afternoon, Papa only sat and held the Bible. No more. He did not open it, and he did not read.

I take out my precious diary to write the events of the

day, but I cannot help but note that there are few pages left bare.

I wonder if our story will come to an end here.

TUESDAY, 5 MAY

This day we leave Yeovil. All of us. Papa, Mother Rodgers, Luther and Cal, all the littles and me. We ride in a wagon pulled by a pair of oxen, carrying us and our meager belongings, the few things we managed to bring from England — Papa's writing desk, the walnut bed, a wooden box of sterling tableware that has long been used to bring scant more than porridge and potatoes to our mouths. Of course, Mother Rodgers's piano is no longer among our belongings. I wonder how she feels about that.

The oxen and the wagon are on loan from Grandfather Chant. He will come and bring back his animals and his wagon when we are settled again.

Papa says that the next town to the west, Glyndon, needs a new pastor, that perhaps he can serve there. Beyond those few words, he has said little.

We bump along through the prairie grass, already begun to stretch tall. I look over at Mother Rodgers and see that her cheek is pale. She closes her eyes, holding one hand cupped gently to her belly. That small gesture allows me to notice what I have not before discerned. We bring more with us from this place than the dust that rises under the oxen's hooves and settles on all our belongings. We bring, too, another little one for our family.

"Will you be well, Mama?" I ask, reaching out to lay a hand gently on her sleeve.

Her eyes startle open, and for an instant she stares at me, as if trying to discern who this be, calling her "Mama." Then a slow smile lifts her face and brings color, once more, to her cheeks. "Yes, daughter," she answers, "I will be well." She nods toward the front of the wagon, though, where Papa walks just to one side, guiding the oxen, and adds, "Perhaps it is your papa who more needs your concern."

I look toward Papa. His steps seem heavy; the reins awkward and unfamiliar in his hands. And just then, while I watch, the oxen lift their great heads, sniff the air and, despite Papa's protests and his fierce pull, they turn out of the track they had been following and take themselves and the wagon and all our possessions and all of us in it toward a nearby pond.

"Whoa!" Papa shouts, trying to dig his heels into the prairie sod. And then "Haw!" But telling them to stop, to turn back into the path, serves no purpose. They only hurry with greater determination toward the waiting water. Once they reach it, they stop at last, their front legs immersed, and take a long, cool drink, the wagon behind them tipping crazily.

Papa's shoulders slump.

I leap down from the wagon, making my way around to stand beside Papa. "They will start up again," I remind him, "when they have had their fill."

"Yes," Papa says, like a child repeating a lesson. "When they have had their fill."

We stand there for a time in silence, watching the oxen drink.

I look around us, noting that the winter's wet has finally dried and that, with it, any patches of earth previously plowed for farming have dried, too. Dried and the topmost part turned to dust. The wind blows, as it always does on the prairie, and the dust is taken up and flung about so that I find myself rubbing at the grit in my eyes.

"I do not wonder," I say, "but that one day, when more farmers have broken the tough sod with their plows, this entire country may pick up and blow away."

But Papa gives no response to my speculation. Instead he asks, looking out across the seeming endless grass, the endless bowl of sky, "Have you heard of 'manifest destiny,' Polly? Do you know what it means?"

"It means," I say, thinking carefully, "that we white people are destined one day to conquer this land."

"Yes," he says. "That is exactly what it means." And for a while he says no more, as though some great question had been answered by our small exchange.

At last the oxen lift their heads, water dripping from their snouts, and allow themselves to be backed away from the pond, to be turned in the direction of Glyndon.

"I think," Papa says when we are moving once more, "that all that seems manifest — easily understood or recognized by the mind — may not, in fact, be true. Perhaps the truth is that we are little more than grasshoppers, flying across the surface of this great land. The prairie itself may have some other destiny in mind."

"But even the grasshoppers populate the earth with their young," I remind him.

"Yes." He sighs. "They do that. But to what purpose? More destruction?"

I do not know what to say. I do not know to what purpose the grasshopper young are hatching from the earth or to what purpose our family sailed across the sea to try to forge a home in this other sea of grass. I know only that this is my papa and that I love him and that wherever he seeks to make a home will be home for me, too.

I look up and see on the horizon, moving on a journey parallel to ours, a cluster of brown hunched backs, wooly shoulders, massive heads. Not the great herds one hears about from not so far in the past, but at least a dozen. Maybe more.

"Look, Papa," I say. "Buffalo. Living buffalo."

Papa looks across the waving grass at the bison and draws himself a little taller as he walks. "Perhaps," he says, "the destruction we bring shall not be entire." And for the first time since we returned from the reservation, he smiles down at me.

"We can only hope," I say, and already I am planning the final words I will write in my small, dear book.

Remembering home

A person can actually *see* the wind in this place. See it starting up a long way off, bending the grass, causing it to ripple and dance, wave upon wave, as though this rumbling wagon were a boat tossed upon water.

And the grass is not only grass, but flowers, too. Wild roses, light pink and dark crimson. Spider lilies. Pink and purple and white daises blossoming in the sloughs. Prairie smoke. Buttercups.

Some of the flowers I do not know by name. There is a great purple flower, for instance, that looks like a miniature Canterbury bell. With or without a name, it grows.

Then there is the loon's crazy laughter. The booming of

the prairie chicken in mating season. The twang of frogs. Geese barking from one end of the sky to the other. Even the wolves' howl is eerie and sweet when one is tucked safely inside a soddy.

The wind, too, sings to us. It whooshes, howls, moans, whispers, pleads, whistles, roars. Unceasing, through every day and night, the wind calls to me.

I look over my shoulder to find our soddy, but it is out of sight. At least it is out of sight of my eyes, but not my heart. I wonder. Will I ever live beneath a roof blooming with flowers again?

Some day I shall have paper and paints once more. Then I shall paint the flowers that bloomed on the roof of our soddy. I shall paint the loon with its red eye and its crazy laugh. I shall paint the grass.

But mostly I shall paint the wind, the constant wind.

When I have paper and paints again, I shall paint myself a picture of my home. Then even if the land forgets we were once here, I will always remember.

LIFE IN AMERICA
IN 1873

EPILOGUE AND
HISTORICAL NOTE

Many of the people you have met here actually lived. I have gathered information about them through oral histories, through correspondence preserved by the town of Hawley, and through names and dates recorded in a family Bible. In the years after the Rodgers family left Hawley, records are more sparse.

For a time, they settled in the town of Glyndon, just a short distance west of Hawley. There Carrie Elva was born, the last of the ten children. But conditions were no better for farmers in Glyndon than they had been in Hawley (or New Yeovil, whichever it might be called). The grasshoppers came again the next year, and an economic recession made cash almost inaccessible in the Midwest.

In January 1876, Dr. Rodgers and his family moved to London, in Ontario, Canada, and in May of the same year to Janesville, near Madison, Wisconsin. The family's last move, in 1880, was to a tiny community called Money Creek in the beautiful bluff region of southeastern Minnesota. There Dr. Rodgers and Emily remained until his death on December 11, 1894. From that time until her own death on April 10, 1910, Emily lived with one or another of her grown children, returning to Money Creek only to be buried next to her husband.

Little information remains about the five children born to Dr. Rodgers's first wife, Mary.

We do know, however, that Mary Ann Elizabeth (Polly), whom I've used as the diarist, grew up to be a nurse. She married, but had no children. She remained close to Elva, the last child born to her father and stepmother, and visited her often after they were both grown.

Elva married and had one daughter.

Percy owned a horse stable and married a doctor whom he used to take on her rounds. They had one daughter born to them and adopted two other daughters and two sons.

Millie married and had one daughter.

Glad became a college professor of mathematics and married, but had no children.

Laura became a teacher in a one-room schoolhouse. She married Orson Hempstead, a forty-year-old bachelor farmer, and they had five children. The fourth, a daughter, was named Elsie. She met Chester Dane while they were both students at Antioch College in Ohio, and after graduation Elsie and Chester married and had two children. The second, a daughter, is the author of this book.

Much of what I have written here is a matter of historical record. My great-grandfather did, in fact, bring a colony from England to northwestern Minnesota. The first members of the colony were greeted with a brass band by the St. George Society in St. Paul. When this first group arrived in Hawley, they were also greeted by an Easter blizzard. They were trapped on the train for some days, burning snow fences and railroad ties to keep from freezing.

It is true, too, that the Northern Pacific Railroad had sent the prospective colonists a map of the town that included both Victoria Park and Albert Square, contributing to the shock people experienced upon arriving to empty prairie. The settlers were shocked also to discover that the land to which they had committed was the beginning of the Great Plains and that there were no trees on it from which to build their homes, a fact that my great-grandfather surely knew, since he had visited the area the summer before, but apparently hadn't thought to mention.

The hardships were heightened by the fact that the men George Rodgers succeeded in inducing to accompany him were mostly tradesmen. They had little understanding of farming or familiarity with any kind of manual labor. One of the colonists actually recalled planting wheat with a dibble. And apart from being inept farmers, they were confronted with numerous hazards, such as drought, hail, fire, severe winters, and plagues of grasshoppers. The grasshoppers, correctly named Rocky Mountain locusts, continued their destruction of great sections of western Minnesota until 1877. That year, for reasons still entirely unknown, the insects rode the wind once more, but never landed.

My great-grandfather Rodgers died before my mother was born, so I have been able to gather from her only a few anecdotes about the actual man, stories passed down to her by her mother. From what I can infer from these stories and from historical records, George Rodgers was a man of large enthusiasms and a golden tongue and no sense whatsoever of the practical. His enthusiasm and his eloquence must have been a great force when it came to gathering a colony, but what was needed, once these people arrived on the Great Plains, was practicality. Though Hawley, Minnesota, the town my great-grandfather settled, remains today, the English colony with which it began can be seen only as a fascinating failure.

Most of what is recorded in this diary is based on actual accounts, either of my own family or of other settlers on the Great Plains at the time. What is entirely created, however, are the people themselves. Even Laura, who became my grandmother and whom I knew in her final years, remains a mystery to me. In fact, because I remember her as a rather dour old woman, ill with Parkinson's disease, I have quite enjoyed turning her into the mischievous child you met on these pages. The truth is, though, that I have little more direct information about these ancestors than my great-grandfather's Bible, given to him by one of his English congregations, which records the birth dates of each of his ten children and the birth and death dates for him and his two wives.

My greatest resource in writing this story was the book *Journey Back to Hawley*, published in 1972 for the town's centennial. Much of my own family's story comes from correspondence and reminiscences preserved in that book. I have compressed the time — the Rodgers family actually remained in Hawley for two years — but tried to remain true to the events. For instance, during the first year Dr. Rodgers received a salary from his congregation; the second year, recognizing the extreme poverty of his people, he refused to accept one, but nonetheless stayed on to serve them.

Dr. Rodgers and his family probably left, not because he was voted out, but simply because the congregation could no longer give even minimal financial support. The antagonism of the community toward their pastor is, however, well recorded. The responses he is quoted here as giving in the church meeting are taken from an actual letter he wrote to answer his critics.

My mother has a few stories of her grandfather. One is of his father's having bought back his apprenticeship — she doesn't know to what kind of trade — so that he could attend seminary instead. He graduated from seminary at age nineteen and for a long time thereafter was called "the boy preacher." Another is of his hair having turned white overnight after his first wife's sudden death. And another is that he was the kind of man who, if he took a few chugs on the churn, thought he had done a great deal of work that day. In other words, we return to the fact that he was not a practical man, which is no surprise, given the golden glow — a glow he himself must have believed wholly — he cast upon this entire enterprise when he was gathering people to accompany him to Minnesota.

"The land is so rich, if you tickle it, it will smile a harvest." Those are George Rodgers's actual words, and though he is not the only one to have used such language in speaking of the Great Plains, he is distinguished, perhaps, for being one who seems to have entirely believed his own rhetoric.

Jane Thompson and her family are imagined, but they are imagined out of the lives recorded by other settlers in this fertile and unforgiving land. I like to think that Jane and Ozawamukwah, who is also imagined, brought many children into the world, children who grew up respecting the cultures of both of their parents and learning to take the best from each.

In May 2001, an article in *The New York Times* referred to farming and building towns on the arid Plains as "the largest, longest-running agricultural and environmental miscalculation in American history." The presence of whites of European descent across the Plains, the article pointed out, is shrinking every year. The population of some counties has fallen below the nineteenth-century definition of land that is vacant or wilderness. These days only the Native American population is growing ... and the herds of bison. "There are now more Indians and bison on the Plains than at any time since the late 1870s."

All of which puts the failed Yeovil colony in perspective and brings us back, perhaps, to Polly's words: "But even the grasshoppers populate the earth with their young." Because these brave people left their comfortable homes to come here, because they tried with such good hearts to make new homes in the face of enormous difficulties, I live ... and my children ... and my children's children ... and, of course, this story lives, too.

Reverend George Rodgers

Emily Chant Rodgers

Laura Rodgers Hempstead

George and Harriet Chant

A street in Yeovil, England, the Rodgers's original hometown.

EMIGRATION.

YEOVIL COLONY.

THE REV. G. RODGERS will sail with Yeovil colonists from Liverpool, on the 25th March. The SECOND PARTY, under the direction of Mr. S. Partridge, of Leominster, will sail in the last week of April.—For information apply to Mr. PARTRIDGE, at Leominster; or to Mr. R. P. CULLEY, Secretary of the Yeovil Association, 226, High-street, Exeter.
[6688.

FREE EMIGRATION TO QUEENSLAND, AUSTRALIA.

Queensland Government Offices,
32, Charing Cross, London.
Owing to the great demand in the Colony for Labour, the

The newspaper announcement that appeared in Yeovil's The Western Gazette *on Friday, March 28, 1873, advertising opportunities to join Reverend Rodgers's traveling party to America.*

210

Immigrants sail from their homelands in Europe to the New World, often experiencing very harsh conditions on the boat, from seasickness to cramped quarters.

The Northern Pacific Railroad maintained a reception house in Glyndon for the colonists immigrating to Minnesota, whom the railroad company sponsored.

A colonist on the Minnesota prairie harvests wheat.

Grasshoppers, also called Rocky Mountain locusts, plagued the Minnesota prairie from 1873 until 1877, destroying crops and eating everything in sight, always riding the wind.

Settlers who lived in sod houses could use the roofs to grow gardens decorated by brightly colored flowers.

Soddies remained quite warm during the bleak Minnesota winters, and refreshingly cool in the summers.

213

An Ojibwa family poses for a formal portrait.

The desolate prairie of Minnesota is filled with sun-bleached buffalo bones.

The graves of Reverend George Rodgers and his second wife, Emily, who are buried in Money Creek, Minnesota.

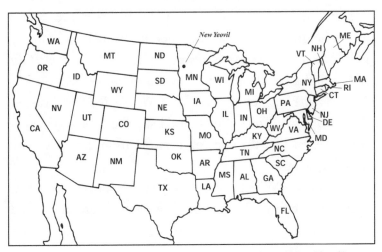

This modern map shows the approximate location of New Yeovil.

ABOUT THE AUTHOR

Marion Dane Bauer is the author of more than thirty books for young people. Her work ranges from novelty books, picture books, and early readers, both fiction and nonfiction, to books on the process of writing, to short stories and middle-grade and young adult novels. She was the first faculty chair and continues on the faculty of the Vermont College Master of Fine Arts in Writing for Children and Young Adults program.

Her books, which have been published in more than a dozen languages, have won numerous awards, including a Jane Addams Peace Association Award for her novel *Rain of Fire* and a Newbery Honor award for another novel, *On My Honor.* Her picture book, *My Mother Is Mine,* was on the *New York Times* Bestseller list. She has received a Kerlan Award for the body of her work from the University of Minnesota.

She says, "When asked to write a novel for Dear America, I had to think about the request carefully. I had never written a truly historical novel and wasn't sure how I felt about the prodigious amount of research required to do so. Finally, though, I agreed, but only if I could use this family story as the basis for my novel. Even when I received permission to do that, however, I still hesitated. After all, I knew nothing more about George Rodgers's colony than a few fragmented stories heard from my mother over the years. I spent a year researching, gathering information about my great-grandfather and his family and the people he had brought with him and stories of other settlers on the Great Plains. I read and read, especially first-person accounts, until I was saturated. By the time I was finally ready to write, I felt almost as though I had lived Polly's journey.

"Writing this story has been a privilege, not just because these people I write about are my ancestors, but because I have lived most of my life on the Great Plains. This land is as much a part of my being as are the settlers who first tested their souls against its promise and its perils. In particular, though, I wrote this story for my mother, who has always been the keeper of family stories. Having grown up on a Minnesota farm, she is closer to this stark and fertile and breathtaking land, even, than I am.

"Mother, here is your family's story. May you savor it long and long."

FOR MY MOTHER,
ELSIE LILLIAN HEMPSTEAD DANE BARKER

ACKNOWLEDGMENTS

Many thanks to Robert A. Brecken, editor of the 1972 Hawley Centennial book *Journey Back to Hawley*. Few communities have so thorough and professional an accounting of their founding and their first one hundred years as that fine book affords.

Thanks to Mark Peihl, archivist of the Clay County Historical Society, for his assistance with photos, and to the McCone family, who built the Sod House B&B, for providing me with a true frontier experience.

My appreciation to my cousin Mabel Jackman, daughter of Elva, the last child to be born into the Rodgers family. She is the only one in the family remaining who remembers Mary Ann Elizabeth Rodgers, and she gave me the gift of the name Polly.

My thanks, as always, to my partner, Ann Goddard, who accompanied me on more than one trip to Hawley, stayed overnight with me in the Sod House B&B, and tromped with me through miles of restored tall-grass prairie, despite a very thorough aversion to snakes.

Finally, I thank my mother, who gave me the foundations for this story.

Grateful acknowledgment is made for permission to reprint the following:

Cover Portrait: Photograph courtesy of the New-York Historical Society.

Cover Background: Photograph courtesy of the Minnesota Historical Society, location no. HD6.43/r104.

Page 209: Portraits of the Rodgers and the Chants, courtesy of Marion Dane Bauer.

Page 210 (top): Yeovil, England, courtesy of Lake Agassiz Regional Library, Hawley Branch.

Page 210 (bottom): Newspaper announcement, *The Western Gazette*, March 28, 1873, courtesy of the Somerset County Records Office, Taunton, U.K., photograph by Richard Sainsbury.

Page 211 (top): Emigrant ship, Culver Pictures.

Page 211 (bottom): Northern Pacific Railroad's reception house for colonists, courtesy of the Minnesota Historical Society, photograph by Haynes Inc., location no. E150 p16.

Page 212 (top): Harvesting wheat, courtesy of the Minnesota Historical Society, photograph by Frank Jay Haynes, location SA4.52 r86.

Page 212 (bottom): Grasshopper plague, courtesy of the Minnesota Historical Society, location no. SA4.9 p55.

Page 213 (top): Soddy roof garden, courtesy of Virginia McCone of the Sod House B&B, Sanborn, Minnesota.

Page 213 (bottom): Soddy in winter, courtesy of the Minnesota

Historical Society, photograph by J. N. Templeman, location no. E200 r97.

Page 214 (top): Ojibwa family, courtesy of the Minnesota Historical Society, location no. E97.1 p10.

Page 214 (bottom): Buffalo bones, Brown Brothers.

Page 215 (top): Reverend and Mrs. Rodgers's graves, courtesy of Willis Dane.

Page 215 (bottom): Map by Heather Saunders.

Although the events described and some of the characters
in this book may be based on actual historical events
and real people, Mary Ann Elizabeth Rodgers is a fictional
character, created by the author, and her diary
is a work of fiction.

All rights reserved. Published by Scholastic Inc.
DEAR AMERICA®, SCHOLASTIC, and associated logos are trademarks
and/or registered trademarks of Scholastic Inc.

Library of Congress Cataloging-in-Publication Data
Bauer, Marion Dane
Land of the buffalo bones : the diary of Mary Elizabeth Rodgers,
an English girl in Minnesota / by Marion Dane Bauer.
p. cm. — (Dear America)
Summary: Fourteen-year-old Polly Rodgers keeps a diary of her 1873 journey from England
to Minnesota as part of a colony of eighty people seeking religious freedom, and of their
first year struggling to make a life there, led by her father, a Baptist minister.
ISBN 0-439-22027-0
[1. Frontier and pioneer life — Minnesota — Fiction. 2. Stepfamilies — Fiction.
3. British Americans — Fiction. 4. Freedom of religion — Fiction. 5. Minnesota —
History — 1858 — Fiction. 6. Diaries — Fiction.] I. Title. II. Series.
PZ7.B3262 Lan 2003
[Fic] — dc21   2002073344

10 9 8 7 6 5 4 3 2 1   03 04 05 06 07

The display type was set in Celestia Antiqua Caps.
The text type was set in ACaslon.
Book design by Elizabeth B. Parisi
Photo research by Dwayne Howard and Amla Sanghvi

Printed in the U.S.A.   23
First edition, April 2003